ONYX NEON SHORTS

HORROR

COLLECTION 2016

Edited By

Jeffrey P. Martin

Failsafe © 2016, Karen Bovenmyer

The Case Yuri Zaystev © 2016, S. L. Edwards

Partisan © 2016, Brit Jones

Sweetie © 2016, Michelle Ann King
Originally appeared at *Drabblecast*, July 2013.

The Corners Have Arms © 2016, Jeremy Hepler

Chestnut Hill © 2016, Joseph Rubas

The Marked Men © 2016, Ben Stallwood

Published by Onyx Neon Press, United States

ISBN-10: 0985451971

ISBN-13: 978-0985451974

First Edition October, 2016

Originally published October 2016

Edited by Jeffrey P. Martin

Cover Art by Jeffrey P. Martin

Designed and Typeset by Jeffrey P. Martin

shorts.onyxneon.com

Onyx Neon Shorts

We are a collective of writers, editors, artists, poets, techies, nerds, and book lovers, who strive to release the best original content.

We publish fiction of all varieties and we are always seeking new authors who also believe in the power of short fiction to express ideas powerfully.

If you have questions or would like to submit a story please email us at **shorts@onyxneon.com**

TABLE OF CONTENTS

INTRODUCTION

JEFFREY P. MARTIN

Last year when the Horror Collection was released we wanted it to be successful and were, as with all things, cautiously hopeful. Once released, we received almost universally positive feedback from readers and reviewers. The book was a big deal for us because we'd never released a collection of horror and had no way of knowing if it would succeed. It became the highest selling project I've ever worked on and continues to sell copies a year later, continuing to garner positive reviews. Without you it wouldn't have succeeded. There's a desire for Indie Horror fiction and we are hoping this one continues that trend. All the support has been humbling, to say the least.

This year is also the last collection I work on and I honestly didn't think I was going to have the chance to make this collection. Due to other commitments I had dropped out of the project. When I was later asked if it would be possible for me to come back in and finish up what I had started. My circumstances and mind set were different and I got excited to come back and delve into the genre I've fallen in love with. Working on Onyx Neon Shorts, Horror Collection 2015 and End of the Year Collection 2014 has been an absolute honor. I've done so much, and have some regrets, but in general couldn't have asked for a better experience. This collection specifically is a special treat because it has a wonderful mixture of new and returning authors who have written seven absolutely wonderful stories that I couldn't prouder to share.

That's all for me, but thank you for buying, borrowing, or stealing this book. I really appreciate it, and I hope that you find something truly disturbing within the pages you are about to read.

Jeffrey P. Martin
Lead Editor – *Horror Collection 2016*
Onyx Neon Shorts

TALES OF HORROR:

Chestnut Hill by Joseph Rubas
A group of people are besieged by demonic beings on a cursed, remote hilltop.

The Corners Have Arms by Jeremy Hepler
When Sophie's ex-husband doesn't return their twin daughters after their week-long visit with him, she fears the worst. Maybe he's kidnapped them, taken them across the border, or worse. She goes looking for her children. If she finds them, will it be worse than she possibly ever imagine? And will she ever make it back?

The Case of Yuri Zaystev by S. L. Edwards
Yuri Zaystev has a thankless job: driving the victims of Stalin's purges into the darkness of the Arctic. One night, something goes horribly wrong. Yuri Zaystev, gulag guard and proud supporter of the purges, finds himself the victim of a violence he helped unleashed.

Sweetie
A travelling showman and his demonic companion teach their latest audience a little respect.

Failsafe by Karen Bovenmyer

Space salvager Kira hates dead bodies. When she finds a lost colony ship, ripe with corpses and a huge finder's payoff, she's happy to report the location and leave well enough alone—until she receives a distress call from a little girl trapped aboard.

Partisan by Brit Jones

Four big game hunters enter the deep woods of a war torn country in search game. It isn't long before they realize that it is they who are being hunted.

The Marked Men by Ben Stallwood

Two men, one recently bereaved, go on a hiking trip in a Norwegian forest. This tale of suicide and loss will leave you breathless and unnerved.

ONYX NEON SHORTS

HORROR

COLLECTION 2016

PARTISANS

BRIT JONES

When the war was over Anderson found himself at loose ends. The Loyalists had lost and, as such, his paycheck had evaporated. Not to mention his welcome in the country. He had heard that there were still partisans operating against the military forces of the new regime, but partisans didn't pay well, if at all, and he hadn't been in it for the cause. There were plenty of brush wars going on around the world, but they all seemed nastier, more primitive, than those to which he had accustomed himself. As an independent contractor he liked more civilized warfare, if there was such a thing. And there was the matter of timely and consistent payment.

Not that money was an issue at the moment. He was in The Bahamas staying drunk and chasing women when he met Blackstock, the scion of a publishing empire and the adult version of a spoiled brat. Nevertheless, he liked the kid. And Blackstock always picked up the check.

They were drinking Long Island Iced Teas on a patio bar at

sunset when Blackstock said, "I'm thinking about signing on to a hunting expedition."

"What the fuck put that idea in your head?" Anderson said.

"There was a guy around earlier, a lawyer, who was talking about putting one together. Sounded interesting."

"Have you even handled a firearm in your short, sweet life?"

"Well, skeet shooting," Blackstock said. "That counts, doesn't it?"

"If you're hunting doves. What's this guy after, anyway?"

"Not doves. Bigger game. Elk. Boar. Maybe even a bear or two."

When Blackstock told him where Anderson choked on the sip he had just taken.

After coughing it out he said, "I was there. Not even a year ago. It's bad, kid. The government's bad. The military's bad. There's still fighting going on in some places."

"Well, this guy said he could get a small expedition in with the new government's approval. He's already got another guy signed on. He needs two more."

"And you're pretty determined to do this, I take it?" Anderson asked.

"It seems kinda like a once in a lifetime chance, don't you think?"

"If you expect your lifetime to be a short one. Let this one go. Wait until you're older and the place isn't a hot spot. You've got plenty of time, as long as your liver doesn't quit on you."

"You've made up my mind. I'm signing on. I'll sit in places

like this and drink myself to death if I don't start seizing opportunities like this by the horns."

"God damn it!" Anderson said, slamming his drink on the table. Blackstock looked shocked.

"Jesus, Anderson, don't get so worked up. It's just something I feel like I oughta do."

Anderson took a deep breath and lit a cigarette.

"Well," he said, "If you've got your heart set on this you're going to need somebody to keep you off of the wrong side of those horns you mentioned."

The airfield was carved out of the deep foliage of the primeval forest and didn't look to Anderson like you could land a remote controlled toy plane on it much less the Cessna in which they were flying. The approach was low, as the whole flight had been.

Under the radar, he thought. *Government approval my ass.*

Still, he had hacked similar airfields out of the forests up north with The Loyalists—you just had to trust that the pilot was skilled enough or crazy enough to put the plane down in one piece.

They hit the ground hard, bounced, and suddenly the Cessna was spinning down the makeshift runway. It finally slid to a halt and the noxious odor of burning rubber filled the cabin. The pilot, decked out in a filthy ball cap and aviator sunglasses, turned around to face them and smiled. He was missing most of his teeth.

"Blew a tire, there," he said. "Everyone okay?"

"You're no Chuck Yeager," Anderson growled.

"Who the hell is Chuck Yeager?" the pilot said.

They had talked on the plane.

"So, Thomas, what are we out here for?" Anderson asked.

"Big game. Trophy hunting."

"Anything specific in mind?"

Thomas seemed stumped for a minute.

"Anything big. Something that will look good over my mantel."

Anderson got a sinking feeling about the leader of their expedition.

They unpacked their gear from the hold of the plane. Other than the lawyer, Thomas, their fourth was Croslin, a taciturn, hulking man who claimed to be a doctor. Anderson instinctively disliked him, but the guy displayed a well-appointed med kit so he went ahead and gave him the benefit of the doubt.

Thomas he liked even less, but more for the man's seeming incompetence than anything else. He was overweight, red faced, and looked stuffed into his expedition outfit. He was sweating in spite of the chill in the air.

Anderson lit a cigarette, ignoring Croslin's dirty look.

"So what are we packing?" Anderson asked.

"Croslin and I have a Springfield .30-06 each. Plenty of stopping power. What about you and Blackstock?"

"I got the kid a .308 Winchester, about the biggest gun he could handle at the shooting range without crying like a baby. For myself, I've used a .338 Winchester Magnum since I got out of the service, and I'm not about to stop now."

"That's a big gun," Croslin said. "We're not hunting elephants."

"Man or beast, I like to be prepared. Speaking of prepared, where's our fucking guide?"

"I wasn't able to communicate a specific time to him," Thomas said. "We'll camp here for now. I'm sure he'll be here by tomorrow night."

"What kind of Mickey Mouse bullshit are you trying to pull here?" Anderson snarled. "A shitty ride on a shitty plane under the radar? A crash landing on an improvised airfield? No fucking guide? I think I want a refund and a ride home."

As if on cue, the pilot, who had been examining the Cessna, stood up and said, "I think she's ruined. I go for help. Meet you here in seven days."

Taylor spluttered, "We only have provisions for five!"

"Then eat what you kill."

With that, the pilot grinned his jagged grin and trotted off down the runway in the direction of what looked like impenetrable forest.

Thomas was incensed. His face became redder than it had been before.

"Why, I'll see that that man never works again!"

"You don't get it, do you?" Anderson said. "You're never going to see that man again."

Their guide, a local to the region who went by Thibault, showed up late the next afternoon. His skin was sallow, almost jaundiced, and what they could see of it from underneath his well-worn garb seemed to hang loosely off his bones. With half lidded eyes, he seemed likely to collapse at their feet. When he took off his cap to brush his hair back Anderson noticed it was patchy and what he could see of the man's scalp was covered with ringworm scars.

"Did you see much action here during the war?" Anderson asked him.

His answer was slow and slightly slurred.

"Some. The Loyalists called us partisans, but we fought only to keep the soldiers from our woods. They withdrew quickly. We've lived here for generations, and strangers are not welcome."

Blackstock said, "Aren't we strangers? I mean, I don't want to go pissing off the locals."

"Stay with me and all should be fine. The Old Ones will never know you are here."

Thomas interjected.

"The Old Ones? Who the hell are they? Witch doctors or something? My contact didn't say anything about hostile natives."

"You are strangers. The less said about The Old Ones is for the best. The rest of us will tolerate you, as long as you listen to me and follow in my footsteps."

"A little uppity for a dirt farmer," Thomas muttered to Croslin, who never seemed to say much.

"Shut your fucking mouth, Thomas," Anderson said.

Thomas was about to reply when he saw something in Anderson's eyes. Muttering to himself, he busied himself with his pack.

"Break camp," Thibault said. "We must be in the woods before dark."

"Shouldn't we wait until morning?" Blackstock said. "It's going to get dark soon."

"Listen to me or do not," Thibault said listlessly. "I tell you it is safer not being out in the open. If you listen you will be safe. If you don't I will return tomorrow, but you may not be here."

"What the hell is that supposed to mean?" Thomas blurted, an edge of fear creeping into his voice.

"Oh, just shut up and listen to the man," Anderson growled. "Try and remember we're guests here. Act like it."

Near dusk, they entered the forest on what was more of a game trail than a path. A few hours later, in the stygian darkness lit only by their lanterns, and after several twists and turns, Thibault finally spoke.

"You sleep here for the night."

"Here!" Thomas exclaimed. "There's not even room to set up tents!"

"There are few places to set up tents on these paths. You must do the best you can. I will return in the morning."

With that he disappeared into the forest.

"Hell of a guide you found there," Croslin muttered.

"We bivouac," said Anderson. "Compared to some of the places I've slept this is a God damned Hilton. I assume you brought sleeping bags."

"Of course we did! We're not idiots,' Thomas declared.

"So far you could have fooled me," Anderson said.

This led to a snort from Croslin and more spluttering from Thomas.

"Shut up and roll out your bags. I'll try and get a fire going," said Anderson.

This went on for two nights. The days were spent trudging through thick, dark and gloomy forest, following Thibault, who didn't seem to be in any hurry. When there was a break in the forest canopy they could see a slate grey overcast sky.

On the second day Thomas testily asked Thibault, "So where's the game? I didn't come out here to wander around the damned woods."

"The game will come. You need to be patient," Thibault said.

"Leave him alone, fearless leader," Anderson said. "Or do you want to wander around this forest for the rest of your life?"

It didn't stop Thomas from endlessly complaining. Anderson wanted to break his neck, and easily could have, but thought it was probably a bad idea, all things considered.

Croslin remained silent unless asked a direct question. Blackstock, clearly terrified by this point, took his cues from Croslin.

At one point he whispered to Anderson, "I think this may have been a bad idea."

Anderson replied, "Just think about how we could be laying around drunk in The Bahamas. That should make you feel worse. And don't forget what I told you when we were there, dumbshit."

"What are you two whispering about?" Thomas practically shouted. "No pussies on my expedition!"

Anderson calmly said, "If you ever speak to either of us like that again I'll kill you where you stand. I'm sick of your whiny shit. And if you want to see a pussy go find a fucking mirror."

Croslin laughed out loud.

Thomas tried to lock eyes with Anderson, but quickly looked away.

Croslin made a rare statement.

"We are in practically trackless deep woods in a foreign country. I, for one, am hopelessly lost and entirely dependent on Thibault to lead us out. Now is the worst time to turn on each other. Anderson is clearly the most capable among us. I suggest we make him the expedition leader."

"Fuck that," said Anderson.

But nobody else spoke and it was decided.

They saw no game. On the third day Thibault did not arrive in the morning. They stayed put that day, waiting. On the fourth day it became apparent he wasn't coming back.

"What the hell do we do now?" Thomas said, clearly terrified. "How are we going to get out of here? We're almost out of supplies."

"First of all, we start rationing. Now," Anderson said. "By my reckoning we've come farther in than out. Thibault has to live somewhere. If we keep heading roughly in this direction we'll hopefully find a village or something like it. Let's take a bearing on the compasses."

But something was wrong with the compasses. They all pointed in different directions, and occasionally spun wildly.

"Shit," said Anderson. "Start hatching trees so we can at least get back this far if things get worse."

The trees did not like being hatched. The bark seemed to recoil from the hunting knives, and the marks looked like they were covering over a few moments of being hatched.

"What's going on, Anderson?" Blackstock said. "You've been here before."

"I was up north. It wasn't anything like this. But there was a war on. Maybe I just didn't notice."

The game showed up that night, shortly before they decided to bivouac. There was a thrashing in the brush by the path and a hunched over form erupted out of it and slammed into Thomas' side. He screamed and went over sideways as the form lurched over him and into the brush on the other side of the path.

Croslin couldn't seem to get his carbine untangled from his pack. Blackstock emptied the magazine on his in five randomly fired shots. The forest roared as Anderson fired three carefully placed shots and was rewarded with a howl on the third.

"You got it!" Blackstock said excitedly. "Let's go look!"

"Thomas first, idiot," Anderson said. "He's wounded. Croslin, I hope you're better with that med kit that you are with that gun."

Croslin gave him a dark look and headed toward Thomas, who was laying in the path groaning. Anderson followed. He looked back at Blackstock.

"You coming?" he said.

"I don't think I want to see."

Thomas' side was torn open and gushing blood. His face was pale and his teeth were gritted. Anderson gave him credit for not moaning and crying.

Croslin was frantically pulling hemostats and a field dressing from the med kit.

Anderson took a closer look at Thomas' side.

"Don't bother, Croslin," Anderson said roughly. "I've seen wounds like that. Unless there's a miracle in that med kit he's not going to make it."

"I have to try."

"You're the doctor," Anderson said, lit a cigarette, and walked back to Blackstock, who had gone from pale to green.

"He's going to die, isn't he?" said Blackstock.

"Yeah, he's going to die. Don't get all weepy. I've seen plenty of better men die for worse reasons."

"You know, Anderson, you're kind of an asshole."

"Yeah, kid, I am."

He crushed his cigarette under his boot.

"Why don't we go take a look at what I killed?"

When they got back Thomas was dead. Blackstock looked more than ever like he was going to throw up.

Croslin was covered in blood and looked like he might start crying. There were two blood soaked field dressings and four blood stained hemostats lying around him.

"I couldn't save him," Croslin said. "I did everything I could."

"I know, big guy," Anderson said. "I told you it was a lost cause."

"Fuck you, Anderson," Croslin said, without rancor.

"Yeah, fuck me. Move over so I can take a closer look at that wound."

After studying it for a few moments he said, "What I thought. Croslin, you're never going to fucking believe what got him."

"What did you kill?"

"Well, that's the thing. I killed Thibault. You better come take a look."

At a distance it looked like a dead boar. As they got closer Croslin realized it wasn't. It was Thibault. He had a boar pelt strapped over his back and limbs. The hooves had been replaced with cast iron claws and he had a metal contraption strapped over his face that had sharp metal tusks where a boar's would be. They were covered with blood, presumably Thomas', as the rest of the blood originated from the large gunshot wound in Thibault's side.

"What the hell," Croslin said. It was a statement, not a question.

"We've obviously alienated these people. In a bad way."

"So what do we do?" Blackstock said. Everything he said sounded more frantic.

"Cool your jets, rich boy," Anderson said. "We've obviously gone and pissed off the locals. I'm pretty sure we can blame Thomas for that. Maybe, hopefully, they just wanted him. All we can do is try and retrace our steps to the airfield. That plane may be ruined, but I bet it's got a working radio. I'd rather be captured by government soldiers than be stuck out here to die."

"What about Thomas?" Blackstock asked.

"We take his supplies and leave him. Unless one of you wants to carry his fat ass."

Neither Croslin nor Blackstock seemed happy about it, but neither objected.

They got Croslin the next night. Just as the expedition had settled into their sleeping bags a large, dark figure dropped out of the trees onto him. The only thing louder than the muffled roaring was Croslin's screaming. It stopped before Anderson could get his gun up and fire two shots, which knocked the figure off Croslin and out onto the path.

Croslin was dead. The blood made it difficult to differentiate between what was the sleeping bag and what was Croslin. The only sound was that of Blackstock being noisily sick in the brush by the side of the path. Anderson went over to see what he had killed.

It was a man, clearly of the same stock as Thibault. He was covered with bear pelts and had long, sharp metal claws attached to his forearms. There was a similar contraption to Thibault's attached to the man's face. He walked back over to Blackstock.

Blackstock was frantic.

"What's happening, Anderson?" he sobbed. "What are we going to do?"

"What's happening is we're fucked. All I can think of to do is find this village and try to talk some sense into these Old Ones Thibault mentioned. Get the med kit. I'll get what supplies Croslin had left. Then we don't sleep until we find these people."

They moved slowly, Anderson in front with Blackstock, quietly sobbing, following close behind. They had their guns locked and loaded. Anderson was using all the skills he had picked up as a guerrilla soldier to watch for traps or ambushes.

He knew they were headed in the right direction when the traps showed up on the path. He carefully disarmed two bear traps and a rudimentary tripwire. It didn't make him feel any better about where they were headed. The only solace he took was that they hadn't been attacked again.

A few hours later they stumbled out of the forest into a ramshackle village. The huts were wood and thatch and looked like they were rotting and sinking into the ground. They surrounded a roofed brick tower that Anderson estimated was about thirty feet tall. He could see a hill with a cave opening in it on the other side of the building. There were stunted, sickly looking people working in dying fields of vegetables.

They were immediately noticed by the closest woman, who hobbled to the tower at alarming speed. A minute after she disappeared into the single door a bell gonged. The rest, consisting of roughly thirty-five people, stopped what they were doing. Still holding their farming implements, they formed a crowd between Anderson and Blackstock and the tower.

"If you can manage it, look mean," Anderson whispered to Blackstock.

The crowd of undernourished yet still intimidating looking people stared sullenly at them. Anderson stared back. Eventually a man, somewhat healthier looking than the rest, shouldered his way to the front. He was holding a rusting bolt action M1 rifle that Anderson judged hadn't been fired since World War II, if ever.

"You are not welcome here," the man said, a slight slur to his voice.

Anderson said, "Yeah, we got the memo. We just want out. There doesn't need to be any more killing. If one of you would guide us back to the airfield you'll never see us again. And you have my word that we won't tell anyone what happened out here. Simple hunting accidents, the way I see it."

A woman shouted, "Thibault was my son!"

Another shouted, "Gregor was my huband!"

"Yeah, shame about that," Anderson said. "But Thibault and Gregor attacked and killed two of my men for no reason. We acted only in self defense."

Anderson noticed that the crowd had completely surrounded them.

"You are not welcome here," the man with the gun repeated. "I will consult The Old Ones. They will—"

Anderson didn't get to find out what The Old Ones might do because Blackstock chose that moment to crack.

"You sons of bitches!" he screamed. "You killed our friends!"

His rifle boomed as he shot the man with the gun, who flew backwards, the old gun flying from his hands.

The crowd roared.

"The tower!" Anderson shouted at Blackstock.

They broke for the tower door, Anderson using the butt of his rifle to clear a path, dodging the farming implements being swung at him. Just outside the door Blackstock shouted in pain as a hoe landed on this shoulder. Anderson grabbed him and pulled him inside. There was a stout wooden door, which Anderson slammed and secured using a makeshift bar. Blackstock was sobbing.

"Let's take a look," said Anderson.

After a cursory examination he said, "Your collar bone

is broken. There's nothing to do for it except strap your arm down, keep it as immobile as possible, and give you some morphine for the pain. I'm not crazy about that last idea, but I don't need you moaning and crying while I figure out what the fuck we're going to do."

The pounding on the door was subsiding.

Anderson opened the med kit and fashioned a splint. There were five ampoules of morphine in squeeze syringes. He took one, jabbed it into Blackstock's neck and squeezed.

About ten seconds later Blackstock said dreamily, "Oh, that's better already." He then leaned over and threw up.

Taking the splint, Anderson said, "Take a deep breath. Even on that dope this is going to hurt like hell."

Blackstock screamed as Anderson strapped his arm to his chest, immobilizing his shoulder. He then gave Blackstock another dose of morphine.

"Try to stay awake," he said as Blackstock's head nodded forward. "It won't be easy but I can't drag you around."

Finally, he explored the space in the dim light. The door was heavy, reinforced wood with the bar they had used across it. It was so lazily constructed he was surprised it had held up under the villagers' assault. Spiraling up into the dim light was rail less stairs clinging to the curve of the tower's wall. A rope dangled down from above, presumably to ring the bell they had heard. Leaning against the wall opposite the door, under the staircase, were two human figures.

Anderson whipped out his hunting knife and crouched, but the figures were still. He carefully approached them only to find two people wrapped completely in corn silk. They were clearly dead. Knowing what he'd find from the shapes of the bodies, he ripped the corn silk from one of the faces. It was Croslin, eyes wide open and a look of terror and pain on his face.

"Well, fuck me," he quietly said. But Blackstock heard him and struggled to his feet and stumbled over.

"Jesus Christ," he moaned, slurring slightly. "Who the hell are these people, Anderson?"

"Don't get hysterical," Anderson answered. "That's not important. What is important is figuring out how to get out of this fucking village, and then the forest, with our skins intact. Do you think you can make it up those stairs?"

Blackstock made it. There was a large bell, its rope dangling down into the dimness of the tower. The platform was open on all sides, a peaked round roof held up by four posts. They could look out at the entire village.

Everything seemed to have returned to normal, the villagers heading back to their meager fields. There was a small group of them around the mouth of the cave in the hill. It was difficult to hear, but they seemed to be chanting.

"It looks like that's where the action is," Anderson said. Blackstock didn't reply. He looked over and Blackstock was leaning against a post, eyes at half-mast.

Anderson slapped him on his injured shoulder, eliciting a yelp from Blackstock.

"I know it's hard, Richie Rich," Anderson growled. "But you need to stay with me. Our lives are on the line. Look.

Something's happening at the cave mouth."

Five preternaturally tall figures, entirely enshrouded in robes, were filing from the mouth of the cave. The villagers there were bowing and moving away backwards.

The figures began to chant loudly, and a mist started coalescing around them.

"So, we finally meet The Old Ones," Anderson said.

"They look tall, not old," Blackstock said, and giggled.

"Christ. Sit down before I knock you down."

Blackstock slumped to the floor, back to the wall. Anderson crouched in such a way that he could glance over it.

"Well, you're the soldier," Blackstock said. "What are the odds for us?"

"Not good, but I've been in tighter situations. Not with a doped up rookie to take care of, though."

"What's the plan?"

"At least you held on to your rifle. Score one for us. Did you bring two magazines like I told you."

"Yeah, two magazines."

"Okay, by my count that leaves you with one magazine after your shooting spree when they got Thomas—you reloaded and shot their head man. One magazine left for me after I took down Thibault and Gregor. Nine cartridges total, but these motherfuckers don't know that. As far as they know we're armed to the teeth."

"Why didn't you take Thomas' and Croslin's guns."

"Added weight and I didn't think we'd need them. There was no way to know we'd be up against a small army of pissed off locals."

"Makes sense, I guess," said Blackstock. "I sure wish we had them now."

Anderson said, "Well, you can shit in one hand and wish in the other and see which one fills up first. There's no point in grousing about it now."

"So what are we going to do?"

"I think the best play is to use your .308 to take out the four of the five freaks, presumably their leaders, which might ruin their morale, then break for the forest. I'll use my weapon sparingly. They won't know I've only got five shots. I think I've figured out which direction north is, so that's where we head. If we make the forest, and with the grace of almighty God, we'll run across a group of partisans, or even a government platoon, before these assholes catch up to us with their animal suits. We'll have to move hard and fast, and stay off any paths as much as possible. It's a long way."

"Why didn't you take Thomas's and Coslin's guns?" He asked again.

"Jesus Christ!" said Anderson. "I think I gave you too much morphine. Just trust me. Go to the bottom of the tower. I'll light these fuckers up and be down in ten or fifteen seconds. We open the door and go. Stay behind me and keep up. Watch our backs. I don't intend to die in this shithole. Now go."

Blackstock stumbled down the stairs. Anderson thought it a minor miracle he didn't pitch off the side. He returned his attention to the action below.

The mist had thickened and taken on a greenish tint. It

was unnaturally holding form and creeping slowly toward the tower. Anderson picked up the .308 and sighted on the figure in the middle who, by this point, was almost entirely shrouded in green mist. He fired, worked the bolt and fired again at the figure on the left, satisfactorily seeing both figures drop. He took down two more of them and ran for the stairs.

At the bottom he found Blackstock leaning heavily against the wall.

"God, it hurts," he said. "We can't leave Thomas and Croslin in this awful place."

"We can and we will. Soldier up, we're losing time. Here, carry this with your good arm and let's get the fuck out of here. Remember to watch my back."

He shoved the exhausted .308 into Blackstock's good hand. Blackstock immediately dropped it.

"Shit," he said. "Hold on. I'll pick it up."

"Fuck it. Time to run, sunshine."

Anderson unbarred the door and threw it open. He went out in a fast crouch, hoping Blackstock was behind him. The villagers were listlessly shuffling toward the tower, forming a crowd in front of them as they came. He shot the closest one and moved forward, using the stock a couple of times to clear a path. Then he fired again, knocking another villager back and down. The crowd stopped closing in and suddenly there was an opening before them.

"Let's go!" shouted Anderson and sprinted through the opening.

He made it about ten yards before he heard the scream.

Looking back, he saw Blackstock belly down on the ground with five tall, robed figures crouched over him. They had begun to turn him over and their claw-like hands were beginning to wrap him in what looked like corn silk. Anderson quickly aimed and let off his final three rounds at the figures. He saw the bullets rip through their robes but none of them fell. One stood up, pointed at him and howled. Anderson found himself running ahead of a mob moving much faster than he would have expected.

"Anderson!" Blackstock screamed. "Don't leave me here!"

Anderson kept running and didn't look back.

CHESTNUT HILL

JOSEPH RUBAS

Harry Parkins shifted in his chair. Murphy, at his feet, lifted his head but didn't move; at seventeen, the hound only moved when he absolutely had to, and when his master showed no signs of getting up, he put his head back down and closed his eyes.

Daryl Morgan, Harry's nephew, closed the magazine he'd been skimming and set it on his lap. The fire in the wood stove was getting low, throwing wild shadows across the walls, and some of the cold autumn wind shrieking outside was starting to seep in. "Are you about ready?"

Without looking up from his book, Harry said, "In a minute."

Daryl sighed. "Come on. We haven't had a customer

in hours."

"Go home then," Harry said, crisply turning a page.

I oughta, Daryl thought, but made no move to stand. Outside, the wind groaned.

The general store, which Harry had owned since 1969, was three miles north of Picketts Meade on Route 29, surrounded by forest. Business was slow during the day, but once the sun went down, forget it. They hadn't had a customer since shortly before seven. It was nine now. Two hours of sitting by the stove, the only sounds the hollow wind and the crackling of the fire. *It's Halloween*, Harry said earlier, *someone might wanna get some candy or something.*

Daryl hadn't been trick or treating since he was ten, but as far as he knew, all that was over and done with by eight-thirty. No reason to stay open now.

"You piss and moan about being tired all time," Daryl said, "but look at you, staying up all night reading."

Harry grunted. "At my age you can't sleep worth a damn anyway. You'll see."

"That why you get up at four in the morning?"

"Yes it is," Harry said.

Daryl rolled his neck. "I'm getting sore sitting here."

"Go home."

"And leave you alone?"

"I got Murphy."

"That dog's as old as you are."

Harry looked up, his glasses reflecting the light of the fire. "If all you're going to do is grouse, go home. I get around just fine without you."

With that, he went back to reading. Defeated, Daryl opened his magazine and flipped to an article he hadn't read yet. He was just getting through the first paragraph when the bell above the door dinged and cold wind filled the store.

Daryl glanced over his shoulder. A man stood just inside the door. Young. Early twenties. He looked nervously around, missed them in their nook, and seemed to anxiously plot his next move.

"Good evening," Harry said, putting aside his book. Murphy, knowing the score, got up and dragged himself closer to the stove so Harry could get up, which he presently did.

The young man jerked, saw them, and smiled. "Thank God. I thought you were closed."

"Nope," Harry said, "we're open. What can I do for you?"

The young man gestured toward the door. "Me and my friends are broke down up the road. We don't have any cell service and I was wondering if I could use your phone."

Harry shook his head. "Don't have a phone."

The young man gaped. "You don't?"

"Harry's too cheap for a phone," Daryl said.

"Never used it anyway," Harry said, spreading his hands apologetically. "You don't have any service here?"

"Let me see." He dug in his coat pocket, brought out a rectangular iPhone, and glanced at the screen. "No." He shook his head. "Weird. We had it coming in."

"This is a bad place for cell phones," Harry said. "Everything from Stonewall to Opal. I can have Daryl here run you into town. They got phones at the police station."

Daryl was sure he saw the blood run out of the kid's face. "Uh...no, that's okay. Really. Could you give me a ride back?"

Harry shrugged. "Yeah, what the hell? We're closing up shop anyway. Where's your car?"

"Chestnut Hill."

Daryl's heart sputtered, and he was sure Harry's did likewise.

"Chestnut Hill, you said?" Harry asked, his voice suddenly uneven.

Sensing their disquiet, the kid suddenly looked worried. "It's not private property, is it? We didn't know. Honest."

Harry and Daryl exchanged a glance. Set back several miles from the road, Chestnut Hill, which rose bald from the sea of twisted trees around it, wasn't the kind of place someone owned. It wasn't the kind of place someone would *want* to own. It was a bad place. An *evil* place. The Indians knew it. They buried their dead there long ago, and as the story went, their dead came back. When white men came along, they laughed at the Indians' superstition. Until their child went missing, and red eyes appeared at their windows at night.

Only stories, of course, Harry and Daryl both knew that. Still...

"No, it ain't private property," Harry said, "but it's not a good place for young people to hang out. Lots of stuff out there, animals and such."

"We'll be out of there as soon as we can."

"Yeah. That's best. Come on. We'll run you up there."

Harry started closing down. Daryl set his magazine aside

and got up. In the bathroom, he pissed, washed his hands, and dried them on a washcloth hanging near the sink. In the mirror, he looked...unnerved. Not scared, just uneasy.

Every town has a haunted house or a haunted road, the kind of place kids tell each other stories about. In Picketts Meade, that place was Chestnut Hill. Standing at the sink, Daryl remembered everything he'd ever heard about the hill and the thick woods around it. Demons. Ghosts walking in the trees at night. Some people said they heard screaming in there. Sobbing. Insane laughter. One old timer when Daryl was growing up said he got lost in there as a kid, said glowing red eyes glared from snarled thickets. "I dunno what that place is all about, but something ain't right," he said.

It's just stories.

Yeah. He knew that. He didn't much like the place anyway, especially after dark.

"You ready?" Harry called.

"Yeah," Daryl said. Shutting off the light, he went into the store proper. Harry and the kid were standing by the door, waiting for him, Murphy sitting by Harry's feet. When he appeared, the trio went outside, Harry holding the door for him. When he, too, was out, Harry shut the door and locked it.

Harry's Blazer was parked along the side of the building, a 1985 model with rust on the hood. Harry coaxed Murphy into the open space behind the back seat while Daryl climbed into the passenger seat and the kid slid into the back. Once Murphy was settled, Harry slammed the tailgate and came around to the divers' side.

"Lotta people say that place is haunted," Harry said, starting the engine. "You ain't seen nothin up there, have you?" He sounded like he was joking, but Daryl thought he was being half serious.

The kid shook his head. "No. It's just strange. One minute the RV's fine, the next...we lost power."

"Like it died?"

They were on the highway now, heading north. The turn off for Chestnut Hill was a mile up, a narrow dirt track nearly hidden by foliage.

The kid nodded. "Yeah. The lights went out and everything."

"Maybe those ghosts didn't like you being there." Harry laughed.

"Maybe," the kid said, smiling wearily.

Daryl didn't think it was funny. Even though he didn't really believe there were ghosts fooling around in the woods, he didn't like the place. He remembered an article he read in a magazine on one of those nights Harry kept him over to the store 'til ten or eleven. It said something about certain places having low frequency sound wave vibrations that caused fear and disquiet in people. One example was a guy working in a lab. Every time the air kicked on, he started getting that ooky, spooky feeling you get when you think a ghost is haunting you. Come to find out, the vent was somehow creating sound waves that rubbed him the wrong way or something. Daryl couldn't remember exactly. It was too science-y for him. But the gist he took away was: some places just scare people. If that was true, then Chestnut Hill was one of those places. Maybe it was the lay of the land. Maybe the hills and trees reflected the wind in such a way it triggered peoples' fear glands. Who knew? Even so, that's not the kind of place for people. Bad environment. Best to just stay away.

By now they'd reached the turnoff. From the highway, the dirt road followed the contours of the land, barreling along a raised ridge through the forest. The trees pressed close, in some points brushing the truck. It was dark in the woods—too dark.

From the storage compartment, Murphy whined.

"What're you guys doing back here anyway?" Harry asked.

"Camping," the kid said.

"You in college?"

"UMW."

That was in Fredericksburg, thirty some odd miles south along the Rappahannock. Nice old town with shaded streets and colonial architecture. Daryl figured the kid and his buddies were out here drinking and doing drugs, like college kids do. Not that he cared. Even now he enjoyed the occasional joint...although it usually put him to sleep.

Ahead, the road bent to the left and disappeared around a gentle hillside. Daryl kept expecting to feel eerie sensations along his spine, but didn't. He felt normal.

After bending, the road emerged from the forest and continued between two barren hills bathed silver in the light of the moon. In actuality, they were the same hill, at least on paper. Chestnut Hill.

"There," the kid said.

About five hundred feet ahead, at the summit, an RV sat in the road. Harry pulled in behind it and killed the engine. "Daryl'll take a look at your RV for you. He knows cars pretty well."

Daryl nodded. "Yeah," he said.

"Thanks," the kid said, getting out. While he jogged out of the along the RV, Daryl looked at Harry. "Thanks for volunteering me."

"We can't just leave 'em up here. Just...look under the hood or something."

Shaking his head, Daryl got out. The kid was just coming out the door along the side. "They're gone."

Daryl stopped. "Gone?"

The kid nodded. "My friends. They're not here."

Daryl's heart skipped a beat. Gone?

"Maybe they went for help," he said.

"I dunno," the kid said, "I don't think..."

Something grabbed Daryl's foot.

"What the shit?" Daryl screamed, jumping back. From the darkness beneath the RV, a blue face appeared, its eyes shining yellow. It reached for him, its fingers long and crooked.

"Give me your liver!"

"C-Cindi?" the kid asked, uncertainly.

Another face appeared from the blackness. This one was male; his face was blue as well. "Mark!" it greeted.

Daryl was frozen. One after another, three more faces emerged from the shadows, hands reaching, grasping.

Cindi was almost fully out, wiggling in the dirt like a serpent. She reached for Daryl's foot again. Daryl jumped back. "If you're friends are joking they better knock it off!"

The kid looked stricken. "Wh-What are you guys doing? Hey."

Cindi went to stand. Daryl kicked her in the face. "Bro!" the kid cried.

Cindi lay motionless in the dust for a moment before resuming her efforts. "I'll eat your toes for that."

Daryl started for the Blazer. "I suggest you come on!" His voice was even, despite his slamming heart.

The kid stood where he was. The things were reaching for him, gnashing their teeth. Realizing something was wrong he started after Daryl.

Harry was standing by the Blazer, the door open. "What's wrong?" he asked.

"L-l-let's just get the fuck outta here!" Daryl said, climbing into the passenger seat.

"What?"

In the back, Murphy was whining.

"What's going on?" Harry asked, leaning in. His face was white. The kid was stopped at the front end, looking back at his friends.

"Get in the fucking car!" Daryl yelled, to both of them.

Harry, obeying, climbed in. The kid started for the door, but something stopped him. Daryl caught a glimpse of his face, and looked back.

Three shambling figures were closing in from behind, their heads crooked and their arms hanging. Harry saw them, too.

"Holy shit!"

"Get in!"

The kid, seeming to snap out of a trance, opened the door and threw himself in. "What the hell's going on?"

Harry turned the key.

The engine clicked.

"Oh no," he whispered.

Daryl looked at him. "Oh no?"

"It won't start."

The figures were closer now. Ahead, Cindi staggered from behind the RV. The others were close behind.

Harry tried again. The engine sputtered but didn't turn over.

"Fuck!"

"Hit the brake!" Daryl cried, hysterical. He popped the brake, and the Blazer started drifting backwards.

Harry spun the wheel. The front bumper slammed into one of the things and knocked it down. The other jerked quickly away; in the wash of headlights, Daryl saw what it was: Its face was skeletal, its eye sockets empty and its teeth jagged and cracked.

They were coasting down the hill now, Harry muttering and Daryl panting. Behind them, the ghouls merged ranks and followed. They were moving fast.

"Harry!" Daryl cried.

Murphy was barking.

The kid was crying.

"I'm trying!" Harry screamed.

The road entered the forest.

They were everywhere: on the hillside and in the ravine, standing stock-still and watching, their eyes red and glowing. Harry saw them, let out a long, low *agggggh*, and lost control of the wheel.

The Blazer drifted left and went over the embankment. Daryl screamed.

It turned over, rolled once, and slammed into a tree, glass shattering and metal crunching. Murphy yelped, the kid screamed, and Daryl yelled. Harry continued gurgling. *Heart attack. He's having a heart attack.*

Daryl's head slammed on the dashboard and for a moment the world went gray.

When Daryl came to, he was out of the Blazer, lying in a drift of dead leaves, the smell of earth strong and pungent.

Shuddering, Daryl got to his feet, nearly losing his balance. The things were coming down the hillside. "I want his stomach lining!" one of them shrieked.

Daryl ran. All around him, eyes watched from the bush. Something came out of the undergrowth, reaching for him. In a cold shaft of moonlight, Daryl saw its face; twisted, black, and doglike, with a long snout and snapping teeth.

Daryl screamed, spun away, and struck out, hitting the thing in its face.

Blind with panic now, Daryl ran, barreling headlong through the forest, branches slapping his rudely in the face. When he reached the highway fifteen minutes later, he was so far gone that he didn't see the oncoming headlights, didn't hear the airhorns.

But he *did* feel the impact.

Sunlight crept tentatively over the land, spreading forth and banishing the darkness. On Chestnut Hill, an RV sat empty. A quarter mile south, a Ford Blazer lay on its side like a wounded animal. It, too, was empty.

SWEETIE
MICHELLE ANN KING

Audiences have so little respect, these days.

Admittedly, my little travelling show isn't what it once was. We've been on the road for such a long time. But I like to think that for the discerning customer, we still provide value for money. An experience you can't get from the computer screen—the modern freakshow—despite all its tricks and special effects.

Of course, it's a different world from the one we started out in. You can't just blow into town, set out your stall and start yelling 'roll up, roll up.' There are rules, now. Regulations. Local councils, who want risk assessments and reviews and background checks—public liability insurance, for fuck's sake.

Time was, I'd parade the streets with Sweetie as a Sumatran tiger padding at my side and grinning at all the fine ladies until they swooned themselves into hysterics. We'd dance with bears and go pickpocketing with monkeys, and everybody oohed and aahed and couldn't throw down their money fast enough. Couldn't wait to see what other wonders I had in store for them.

But those days are gone, now. Instead of wild animals I have beetles and cockroaches and corn snakes—and Sweetie, of course, I still have Sweetie.

We don't parade the High Street now, or line people up outside a huge, gaudy tent. We travel in a Transit van and squat temporarily in vacant outlets sandwiched between charity shops and Poundstretchers, and hide from Community Support Officers on the lookout for unlicensed traders.

But for all that so much has changed, some things—some people—never do.

It's not the kids—they're fine. I like the kids. They're excited, wide-eyed, thrilled to get up close. They love Sweetie, even when they're pretending to be scared, and she loves them right back. Lets them stroke her back, her legs, with shivering fingertips.

'She won't hurt you,' I tell them, and they usually grin and nod and pose proudly for mum or dad to take a video with a smartphone. But they're still ever so careful with her. They respect her. Because deep down they know—I can see it in their eyes—I might be lying to them. And that's good. That's a worthwhile lesson for them to learn.

So no, it's not the kids. It's the ones who think they're adults, tough guys; the ones who think that because they've seen the world on a screen, they know how it works; the ones who think if there's anything to be scared of, it's them.

Bless their hearts. Bless their deluded, juicy, little hearts.

'No,' I tell this particular tough guy. 'I wouldn't recommend that.'

He blinks at me. We're in a seaside town, for some reason a place that attracts these roaming hordes of young men, sloshing around in clouds of alcohol fumes and testosterone. Time was they'd have ended their nights out by being press ganged into service on a Navy warship. These days they tend to get swept out of disreputable nightclubs in the cold hours with the rest of the rubbish. But either way, the middle of the spree has to be filled with fun. Specific definitions of that word might have evolved over the years, but the general translation of "trouble for someone else" hasn't changed much.

'Fuck you,' he says, this little pumped-up runt. 'I want to hold the fucking spider.'

I give him a pondering look, making a show of it. 'I'm not sure,' I murmur. 'The tarantula experience can be a little intense. Perhaps I might suggest...?'

He follows my gaze to the glass case of stick insects, and his eyes bulge almost as much as his biceps. His companions snigger. Do people still die of apoplexy in this age? I hope not. It would be wasteful.

'Are you kidding me?' he says.

I attempt to assure him that I am not—that I am thinking only of his safety and welfare. It doesn't seem to soothe his ire.

He looks at the poster on the wall, a blown-up photograph of Sweetie sitting on the outstretched palm of a previous customer.

'That kid is about six years old,' he says. 'Are you saying six-year-olds can handle it and I can't?'

One of his friends slaps the back of a hand against his upper arm. 'Fuck it, Chris, let's go.'

'No,' he says, and points at me. His fingers are square and chunky, yellowish staining on the underside. I would have blamed nicotine, once, but I suspect it's more likely a tanning solution. 'I want the spider. It's the only reason we came in here in the first place. You said people can hold it, so I'm going to.'

I compose my expression into reluctance and take a typed disclaimer out of a plastic tray on the side. He slaps it out of my hand and it drifts to the floor. Perhaps that's just as well; it's a prop, like the fake bamboo in the cases, and makes no sense whatsoever. Although I'm not sure he would realise that even if he read every word.

'I won't sue you,' Chris says, the words barely getting out through clenched teeth. 'I might nut you one if you don't stop fucking me about, but I won't sue you. All right?'

'Fuck's sake,' says the other young man. He looks jittery, pulling on the collar of his shirt. There are sweat stains spreading out from under the arms. 'Can't we just leave it?'

Maybe it's chemical, this edginess—maybe he just wants to rush off towards the next fix of his regular poison. But there's something in his eyes that reminds me of those sensible children who knew when to be scared. Maybe this one really does understand something of the world, after all.

The rest ignore him. I get the impression Chris usually puts on a good show, and they don't want to miss anything.

Good for them.

Sweetie currently lives in a five-gallon aquarium, the bottom layered with a few inches of soil and peat. She has a shallow water dish and a cave in the form of a small clay flowerpot. I remove the lid and lift her out.

The men fall into a semicircle and lean in closer. There's a very small noise, little more than a vibration, but it almost sounds like an 'ooh.' A warm rush of nostalgia sweeps through me.

'What do you feed it?' a member of the chorus asks.

'Crickets,' I lie.

Sweetie sits on my palm, unmoving. You could imagine she was just a model, a toy—maybe a corpse. She plays dead extremely well.

'Hold out your hand,' I tell Chris.

For a heartbeat or two he hesitates—vestigial survival instinct, perhaps. But if so, it's easily overridden. He won't back out now, not after so much fuss. In this modern world, social embarrassment is a far greater fear.

He pushes back the sleeve of his shirt and offers me his hand. I bring mine next to it until our fingers brush. His flesh is cold, but he still jumps, minutely. Perhaps mine is colder.

I tilt my hand and Sweetie tumbles fluidly from my palm to his. He stiffens, the muscles in his arms and his jaw visibly rigid. Another whisper of sound; the complementing 'aah.'

We all wait.

She moves a foreleg, taps it gently on his skin. 'She's reading your palm,' I say. 'Telling your future.'

They all smile, as if I've said something funny. Chris breathes out for the first time in at least thirty seconds, and then frowns.

'Is it supposed to do that?' he says, because Sweetie's changing her colouration. Amber bands are appearing on her legs, reminiscent of the Mexican Red-Knee—probably because that's the classic image so often used in illustrations and films. Say 'tarantula' to most people and that's what they'll think of.

'She likes you,' I tell him.

I don't always lie.

He raises his hand and brings her up to eye level. 'You're not so scary,' he says.

The blond boy in the stained shirt winces and closes his eyes, and I know that he's seeing Sweetie jump, legs extended and fangs bared—fangs that make no sense for a creature that size. He'll be seeing these things in his dreams for a long, long time.

But at least he'll wake up, afterwards. He has that advantage over his friend.

Sweetie and Chris are still eye-to-eye. The others are getting restless; it doesn't look like there's much more fun to be had here.

'Are we going?' one of them says.

'Yeah,' Chris says, but he doesn't move.

'Catch us up, then, yeah?'

They're drifting towards the door now, listening to a different siren song. The blond is the first one out, his face ashen and his chest heaving as he gulps polluted street air as if it tastes fresher than inside the shop. The others laugh, thump him on the back and call him names.

'Yeah,' Chris says again, but they've all gone.

We have to go too, now. They'll come back for him eventually. Or they'll remember that he was here, at least—that this was the last place they saw him.

I pack everything up quickly and neatly, leaving nothing but dust and whispers. I still miss the romance of the covered wagon, but it has to be said that the van is a far more efficient method of transport.

I slam the back doors on Sweetie and her new friend. I think Chris would be screaming if he was still capable, but he'll settle soon enough. We'll head out to Eastern Europe for a while, I think, somewhere that hasn't entirely sacrificed awe and wonder for regulations and small print. He should be ready, by then, to take his place as the star attraction of my little travelling show. Sweetie doesn't mind sharing the limelight, sometimes. She's good like that.

FAILSAFE

KAREN BOVENMYER

I don't like ships with corpses.

I don't mind a salvager's life—the time alone, the long hours searching—but ships with bodies, those bother me. Shake me up for weeks after, sometimes, almost aren't worth the nightmares. Some of my fellow salvagers climb aboard wrecks and work over the dead for anything valuable because TerraCo lists unfound personal effects as lost or destroyed. Not me. I can't rifle corpses and stay sane. When I find a ship, all I want is my fee. Someone else does cleanup. I don't need anything held by the dead, and I like my ship's cozy little bridge just fine. My next move after finding is always to submit the coordinates and head toward the core worlds to collect my big TerraCo payoff. But this time I waited, fighting a lingering feeling like there was something I was supposed to do. I tried to ignore it, but I couldn't shake it off. The colony ship revolved in the dark like a ruptured beehive, circled by a nimbus of empty lifeboats. Thirty-foot letters—*The Eden Queen*—marched unbroken across her bulbous midsection, but the lower half of the hulk was breached by a crescent grin. My searchlights picked up a glint of twisted metal shining back from the scar—whatever violence had rendered the *Queen* lifeless had been explosive and quick.

"Everyone's dead—" A voice from nowhere spoke. I jumped, my twitch jerking the camera focus into empty space. Nothing but black—not many visible stars this far out on the rim.

"Hezu, *Recovery*. You fekken scared me," I said.

The nowhere voice replayed in the air like someone singing in another room. *Everyone's dead—Everyone's dead—Everyone's dead—*

I cracked my knuckles to hide a sudden case of nerves that made my hands shake—the AI monitored my health constantly and got preachy when she thought her captain was straining herself. Dry-mouth scared probably counted.

"I'm sorry, Kira," my ship said. "You told me to play transmissions coming from the *Queen*. This is the only one."

"Everyone's dead—"

The words cycled again, clipping off each time as though the speaker were interrupted.

"Analysis—adolescent female between the ages of nine and thirteen. High levels of stress," *Recovery* said.

"No shit," I said. The message had been little more than a terrified whisper. I've never been a mother—that ship left port years ago—but even I could hear the trauma in that kid's words. "Play the rest of it."

"There isn't any more, Captain. The transmission repeats." *Recovery's* reasonable, clinical voice switched to the kid's in a heartbeat.

"*Everyone's dead—*" she repeated. *Recovery* let it cycle for a minute and the small voice floated from the speakers, alone and afraid.

"Shut it down. You're making me jumpy."

The AI complied, leaving me in silence, which was almost as bad. Over fourteen hundred colonists had been aboard the *Queen*, heading out to a new rock on the rim with a belly full of terraformers. Now only this one voice sounded in the dark—surely the person who belonged to it was long dead. That little lost voice reminded me death waited for us all, and the departed made me nervous. I've seen enough deep space to know there are things beyond our understanding—we salvagers talk to each other, and there's a drunk in every port yarning about haunted ships sailing themselves, proceeding on to some unknown place for purposes of their own. Whatever you may think about those washed up spacers, I know as sure as vacuum that there are things in the black, waiting, that collect all the souls we leave out here. An odd belief for someone who combs the stars for salvage, but there are things even I don't like to mess with. The dead are one of them.

"The data is incorrect." *Recovery* interrupted my thoughts. She was always doing that—she was programmed to keep me company and didn't like long silences.

"What are you talking about?"

"Everyone is not dead."

"Obviously the kid had to be alive to record the message. That doesn't mean she's alive now," I said. Damned literal AIs.

"But someone *is* alive aboard the *Queen* now, Captain."

"Show me," I said. The colonizer had been lost with no contact for the last sixty-seven days. I'd only been looking for her for forty. Spending a few weeks in a pilot's chair was pretty natural for someone like me, with quadrants to search and places to be. It was something different trapped aboard a failing ship among hundreds of decomposing bodies, not knowing if the next breath would be your last.

"The *Queen's* AI is not answering my hails, but I have accessed rudimentary data. One of her redundant cores is active." *Recovery* took over the viewer, which re-centered on the *Queen*. Sensor data graphed across the image of the stilled ship, reporting her energy stats and the soundness of her hull. Despite the rip in her shell, the *Queen* had functioning oxygen, heat, and even gravity. *Recovery* scrolled the crew manifest:

Captain Daniele Marachisio: <u>deceased</u>

Operations Manager Wilhelmina Lymari: <u>deceased</u>

TerraCo Engineer Giacomo Quinquilleros: <u>deceased</u>

Crew Coordinator Yergi Serchenko: <u>deceased</u>

"Okay, you can skip to the interesting part any time now, *Recovery*."

The names floated up, all listed by their command tree aboard the big TerraCo colonizer. I told her to speed up the scroll until they were little more than a blur. Then she stopped.

"Juvenile Elizabet Lovara, cargo deck A, section C," she read aloud.

"The transmission—is that voice hers? Adolescent female?"

"It could be, Captain. At that age, voice print identification is not one hundred percent viable."

"Give me your best guess then."

"Yes, Captain. The match is likely."

Sixty-seven days with no contact. Sweet baby Hezu. "When was the transmission sent?"

"Thirty-two days ago."

I cracked my neck to suppress the feeling of cold fingers along my spine. Still alive a month after sending that terrified message—weeks of living with rotting corpses on a partially functional ship, breathing air fouled by the dead, saving up whatever hope remained to get through the next few minutes, hours, days—a child alone.

"I have prepped for boarding, Captain."

"Hellfire and damnation." I really, really did not want to go aboard the *Queen*. I wasn't equipped for this situation, but *Recovery* was right to prep. Aid-and-assist was in my contract; I was bound by law to confirm any survivors and help them. I watched the *Queen* revolve across the view-screen and wondered if saving Ms. Elizabet Lovara from her situation was possible. Even if I brought her back to TerraCo's team of skilled psychs and medtechs she'd have to live with those sixty-seven days forever. Maybe she'd never escape the *Queen* no matter where her physical body was. But *Recovery* played the ghostly, lost little voice again, and I climbed out of my pilot's seat and put on my EVA suit.

EVAs always make me sweat like hell, and I itched as I waited in *Recovery's* claustrophobic airlock. The *Queen* didn't make it easy on me either—the explosion that had ripped a smile in the ship's plating had warped her pressure hull so most of her airlocks were fekked. *Recovery* couldn't get a seal on the first three, and I felt as much as heard the pressure from the next two seals lock tight, but neither would open. By the time we finally pressurized into our sixth, my hands were slipping around in my gloves and my faceplate was fogged. The CO2 scrubbers did what they could to regulate moisture, but couldn't keep up. At last, the gray metal of the *Queen's* outer lock slid away, and I looked through the tiny window down the throat of a long, dark hallway. There were no blue-lipped dead staring sightlessly back.

"Calm down, Captain." *Recovery* said. "Your heart rate is accelerating beyond the recommended coherence zone."

"Thanks. I'll get right on that." I took a few deep, shaky breaths and checked my vitals again. "Just open the door."

"Yes, Ma'am."

The door whooshed open, and the low-pressure inside the *Queen* sucked the air from the *Recovery's* lock and pulled me forward a few steps, off-balance in my clunky EVA boots. The humidity change filled the small space with swirling fog.

"Oh, that's not eerie at all."

"What do you mean, Captain?"

"Never mind."

"Check in periodically, if you are able. Communications disruption is likely."

"Great," I said. I hadn't walked anywhere in an EVA in years. Hell, I'd barely bothered changing out of my pajamas for the last month, much less kept up with security drills like I should.

Recovery kept the lock open behind me, lights as bright as she could make them, and I took a few echoing steps into the *Queen's* labyrinthine bowels. "Can you do anything with the AI? Turn on the emergency lighting?"

"I'm trying, Captain. Something is wrong with my counterpart. She has been deactivated. My probes are encountering holes—vital components have been destroyed or removed. I can access some data from abandoned sub-cores, but I do not have system control."

"Destroyed? Is that even possible?" AIs, by rule, had multiple failsafes—the redundant systems had redundant systems and their cores were spread throughout every operational routine. A big colonizer like this would need one hell of an AI, and if she were gone—the damage must have been worse than it looked.

Then I realized the kid didn't even have an AI to keep her company. *Hezu*, she was going to be in bad shape. I adjusted the strap on my toolkit and wondered what I would do if she were genuinely space mad. It happened sometimes; too much time alone and a survivor forgot how to be human, how to talk, or even that they had once been a person. The crew being rescued sometimes attacked salvagers, and I suddenly wished

I hadn't left my gun under the pilot's seat on *Recovery's* bridge. Stupid, but going back for it would mean going through decontamination and taking off my EVA. Maybe this would be easy; maybe I'd just get the kid and come back and we'd be on our way. And maybe I should buy an asteroid diamond mine from a guy who won't show me his face in the next port.

"Is Lovara still in Cargo A?"

"Yes."

"Any idea what she's doing?"

"I'm sorry, Kira. I cannot access system control. There are no camera feeds."

"Fine." I took a deep breath and started walking, my boots echoing down the long hall and my shoulder lights bouncing ahead of me like distant stars that never got any closer.

It'd been a long time since I'd walked a ship this big, corridors branching every which way. I called up the schematics on my viewpad and traced the layout of corridors between me and the big cargo holds in the *Queen's* belly. The inside of my gloves were so slick I almost dropped the viewer. I double-checked the *Queen's* atmospheric readings—tolerable oxygen and temp—so, when I stopped to rest at a junction, I opened my faceplate.

"Captain, I recommend keeping your atmospheric seals intact. My analysis estimates some compartments are depressurized."

"Thanks, *Recovery*," I said, and ignored her advice. "You'll warn me when I get to those." The air was cold on my moist face and neck, and the *Queen* smelled like burnt matches and old skin. I unsealed my gloves. It was a relief to be able to feel things with my fingers, even if I left wet prints on the view-pad. The light of the *Recovery* grew fainter behind me and my breathing echoed in the corridor—it curved ahead out of sight. I turned around for a last look at home and comfort and was reminded how limited my range of motion is in an EVA suit. *Recovery* waited, but I walked down the corridor anyway.

The shoulder lights of my pack showed black licks of carbon on the ceiling, walls, and closed doorways as I passed. There had been a fire aboard. Standard procedure would be to close bulkheads and vent the air in the affected compart-ments—I guessed that was why the *Queen* had damned near sucked me out of the *Recovery* when I opened the lock—the result of cold air and low pressure in the compartments that were still sealed.

The first double-thick bulkhead door was closed. Coloniz-ers had several atmospheric pressure bulkheads, because they were made to enter a planet's envelope and terraform up close and personal. Scorch-marks rimmed the door, and the control panel had been pried off, so I put my EVA gloves back on to poke around in the jumbled tangle of hanging wires. It still had juice, but someone had bypassed the AI so power fed di-rectly to the opening mechanism. A clumsy job—I suspected the kid, even though the knowhow should have been beyond an adolescent, even a career spacer like a colonial.

I pinched two wires together, and the door screeched start-stop open, revealing a dark hole beyond, one slice at a time. My light crept inside, and then the smell hit me. I realized what the lumps on the floor were when burnt meat and the rot of decomposition invaded my nose and lungs. Bodies. I breathed out hard and slammed my faceplate down, hoping the scrubbers would help when I had to breathe in again. They didn't, and worse, my fogged faceplate was slow to clear. Knowing the corpses were lying there in the dark without being able to see them was worse than smelling them, but when the plate cleared I wished it hadn't. I counted about thirty and reported those to the *Recovery*. Every one of them was fuel for nightmares.

"I'm sorry, Kira."

"Thanks." Programmers give limited AIs, like *Recovery*, rudimentary sympathetic responses, but when she said stuff like that, it felt hollow. No feeling behind it. The lack of sentiment helped me keep my voice steady. "Log those officially. They're in uniform—mostly engineers. Map shows engineering's on the other side of this corridor. They were probably trapped in here when the air was vented to put out the fire."

"Captain, your heart rate is—"

"Can't help it. Don't tell me about it."

"Yes, Ma'am."

I wanted to close the door again, go back to the *Recovery*, and leave. But the kid was on the other side of those bodies. I turned up my air so it blew out of the collar of my suit and sent hair tickling across the back of my neck. I stepped over the threshold and picked my way through the bodies using my unsteady shoulder-lights to see by. Some of the corpses were scorched, so that was good. The cooked parts weren't as hard to look at. The others were oozing—there wasn't much skin visible, thank Hezu for modest uniforms, but what I could see had purpled in death. The faces of those bodies were rot-melted masks, no longer distinguishable as human, all sunken eye-holes and slit mouths. They were featureless, like poorly made dolls. I called out the names I saw on the lapels for *Recovery's* report. Some of the skins had burst, pooling liquid out of the uniforms onto the floor. The cold air in the ship had kept them from decomposing as fast as they might have, but hadn't preserved them enough. I stepped as carefully as I could, but I couldn't avoid getting some of the slop on my boots.

"Captain, you must stop. Your cortisol levels are above the recommended safe threshold."

"On the other side."

But when I reached the door at the end of the corridor, it wouldn't open.

"*Recovery*, any luck with the *Queen?*" I knew she was tracking me like she had the girl in Cargo A. "Can you open this door?"

"I cannot access system control."

I had a hard time opening the panel, particularly because I was shaking and sweating so much I was afraid of dropping my tool. If I dropped it, I fek-all wasn't picking it back up again. The insides of the control panel were scorched and burnt. The fire had disabled it, melting wires; there was no chance of it opening.

I'd have to go back through the bodies.

"Captain, I highly recommend you cease strenuous activity."

"Shut up, *Recovery*." I picked my way back through, trying to put my feet down without looking at the slowly liquefying corpses. I couldn't help but notice every one had twin pools leaking out of the wrist cuffs. Halfway across, I realized they didn't have hands.

I stopped and took a long, slow look that left me dizzy, panting in shallow gasps.

Handless. Every one. As though someone had cut them off.

"Captain?" *Recovery* actually sounded a little alarmed.

"I'm okay."

"The data disagree."

"I'm all right. I just noticed something about the bodies, that's all." I spared her the gory detail. The room seemed to hold a hush that didn't want to be explained. "I'm getting out of here."

After I closed the first door behind me, the empty corridor of the *Queen* felt almost cozy. Something splashed—I looked down—putrefying liquid had pooled out of the room and trickled down the hall. I wanted to take off the boots even more now, but settled instead for turning up my air to full. It didn't save me from what I'd already breathed in, which seemed to have taken up permanent residence in my nose. I consulted the map. I could get to cargo by going around engineering, up a few decks above where I'd seen the explosion that had breached the hull, then back down. Or I could get a laser torch from *Recovery* and cut through the door I'd just tried, but I didn't want to repeat what I'd just experienced. Not ever.

Even though I knew I would anyway on long, sleepless nights. So, around and over it was.

The first lift I came to was disabled, but rather than go looking for another one, I took an access ladder. It felt good to climb up and away from the bodies, like I was escaping them somehow.

I ran into another locked door when I tried to cut across the decks. "Can you hear me, *Recovery?* I'm at a dead end."

"Yes, Captain." Her response was broken with static. I'd passed the first atmospheric bulkhead, and it was already interfering with the signal. "If you go to the bridge and activate the AI's communication module, I may be able to assist your navigation."

"My only goal is to find that kid and get us off this hulk."

"I know, Ma'am, but I will be able to maintain communications if I can tap into the *Queen's* systems. I am uncomfortable with the amount of strain I am detecting in your vitals, Captain. You are no longer a young woman."

"Thanks for the reminder. And fifty ain't old."

"After fifty years of age, stress tolerance rates are decreased by—"

"Fine. I'll go to the bridge if you stop telling me how old I am. Shut up already."

"Yes, Captain."

As much as I didn't want to admit it, the AI was right. I wasn't young anymore, and even though I spent the required time on the exerciser every day, I didn't exactly lead an active lifestyle. The bridge of the colonizer was at the head of the beehive, so to speak, and that was a long, long climb.

After what felt like an eternity of listening to my own echoing breaths, I stopped to rest. My boots still stank, but I felt cleaner after the exertion. It was tempting to stop at crew quarters on my way to use the head, but I had no idea what I might find there. I didn't want a repeat of what happened in that corridor. And my knees ached.

"Talk to me, *Recovery.*"

"Yes, Captain. Are you making progress?"

I consulted the map. "Over halfway there. Any changes?"

"Unsure."

"What do you mean, 'unsure'?"

"The data are in fluctuation."

"What do you mean? What fluctuation?"

"TerraCo Engineer Giacomo Quinquilleros is in Cargo A."

"No, he's not. I stepped over his remains. You don't forget reading a name like Quinquilleros off a lapel badge."

"I'm sorry, Kira."

"Don't be sorry, *Recovery.* Be accurate. Don't tell me I'm going through all this for nothing. Is the kid fluctuating data too?"

"No, Ma'am. Juvenile Elizabet Lovara is two decks below you, in crew quarters."

"What? Why didn't you tell me she'd left Cargo A?"

"You told me to shut up, Captain. I thought it best not to disturb you."

I swore. Damned literal AIs. "She moves, I want to know

about it."

"Yes, Captain. She is in crew quarters, heading in your direction."

Cold knuckled up the back of my neck again. I didn't want to be caught on a ladder in a tube by a kid who might or might not be totally mad. Fluctuating data or not, someone had cut off those hands.

I climbed off the ladder at the next hatch and tried the panel. No power, like the others, so I pried open the cover as fast as I could and twisted wires together. It slid up, and I went through another pressure bulkhead.

For the first time I was inside a room that had its own source of light—flickering blue emergency beams and a couple of spotlights on tripods trailed cables into an open power interface. More panels were off the walls, wires dangling down. There were steel tables, cabinets, and open crates of foodstuffs. I checked the map. Galley. I looked down the access ladder. No kid. I shut the door and looked for something to defend myself. I rifled through two drawers, one full of spatulas, the other oven mitts, before *Recovery* interrupted me, her words partly blocked by static.

"Captain . . . has . . . sec . . . Lovara . . . closing . . . your current . . . ."

I got the gist. "Which way?"

" . . . through . . . mess hall . . . several . . . . "

I looked—the steel portals between the galley and the mess stood opposite a set of glass doors, probably refrigeration or freezing units. They'd be an ideal place to hide even if they were cold, because I was in an EVA with its own heat source. I picked one and ducked inside, sliding closed my faceplate to muffle anything *Recovery* might manage to transmit. I'd chosen a freezer with frosted boxes jumbled across the floor and rows of narrow shelving stacked high with slim packages. I backed up and crouched down, shutting off my lights just as a glint bounced off the galley door swinging in.

Someone walked through it. She was small, about four feet tall, wearing an EVA for juveniles with a bubblehead helmet, faceplate closed. She paused, looking around the galley. Her arm raised—she held a long knife that reflected the blue emergency lights, and she walked straight to my freezer door. I scrambled back, looking for anything for defense. I grabbed one of the packets from the shelf, intending to throw it. It felt wrong in my fingers. I looked down.

It was a human hand.

" . . . . . . current activity . . . heart," *Recovery* said as I dropped the grisly package and the kid opened the freezer door.

Her EVA was streaked with dirt, oil, and other fluids I didn't want to identify. She pointed the knife. I held up my hands—the universal sign of peace, I hoped. Then again, maybe not for this kid.

She lifted her faceplate. Her kinky black hair clung in sweaty curls to a delicate face with prominent cheekbones. Her dark skin was ashen and her brown eyes protruded—like she was suffering from malnutrition and probably hadn't spent time under a vitamin D lamp in a while. I said the first thing that popped into my head.

"Don't stab me."

"You stupid! You let him out and I was almost done!" I thought maybe her voice was the same I'd heard aboard the *Recovery*, hoarse and strained, but this time angry instead of afraid. "You don't open doors. Never."

"Okay." I kept my hands up, because she still had the knife. She was short but she looked like she was thirteen or fourteen.

"Come out. Now." She held the door open. She didn't lower the blade, but kept it pointed at me, like holding it out and ready was a habit.

I moved slow and steady, nothing sudden, racking my brains for anything useful. I'd watched a space madness training vid about twenty years ago when I'd gotten my salvager license, but now the memory of it was like a missing tooth. Something had been there once, now, nothing. I approached her, and her little turned-up face watched me with predatory care. I slid past her, my eyes never leaving the blade, and she followed me into the galley proper.

"You're Elizabet, aren't you?" I said in my calmest voice, the one I reserved for other people's mean-spirited pets.

"You call me Walkabout." She lowered the knife, and I felt a tiny surge of hope swoop up my chest. Maybe she wasn't totally gone.

"I'm Kira. My ship's the *Recovery*. I'm going to get you out of here."

" . . . Captain . . . data . . . ." *Recovery's* voice garbled up from my comm.

"Who's that?" She pointed the knife again.

"It's okay, it's just my AI—"

"No! You have to turn her off!"

"She's okay, Walkabout. She's going to help us."

"No! He can get her. It will take him a while, but he can get her. Then he'll get away. You have to get off." She fished a viewer out of her EVA's thigh pocket, her eyes still on me, wary. She glanced down at it. "He's moving. Hurry up."

She slid the knife into a crude plastic sheath hanging from her belt, ran to the tunnel with the ladder, and disappeared through the hatch. She reappeared in a moment. "Hurry, you stupid. I don't have any codes for your ship and it's hard to get the hands off while he's in someone, only after he gets out. You gotta help."

I stared at her.

"Hurry up. We need to go back to your ship. Now." Then she disappeared again.

I had no idea what she was talking about, but going back to the *Recovery* was what I'd wanted to do since coming aboard, so I followed her.

She was quick, way faster than me. She slid down the ladders with the practiced ease of someone who did it every day. I panted like a ventilator, turning my suit lights on and doing my best to keep up.

"Captain, report. I am concerned."

I'd never been happier to hear my AI's static-free, emotionless voice. "*Recovery*, go into lockdown. Do not allow anyone on board, do you hear me?" I knew everyone on the *Queen* was dead, and the kid was probably raving, but I didn't want to take any chances she might be right about another survivor wandering around.

"Yes, Captain. Standard procedure dictates lockdown after crew departure. I have been in lockdown since you boarded the *Queen.*"

"Hezu bless you." At least *Recovery* followed standard procedure, if I didn't. "Let's keep it that way."

"I'm sorry, Kira. That may not be possible."

"What do you mean?" I was out of breath, and the kid opened a hatch and went through, one deck below where I thought the *Recovery* was docked.

"Someone is attempting to access my core."

"What?" I stopped, gripping a rung tight. The AI's core was her central brain and what kept every part of the *Recovery* functioning, from the wave drive to the life support. She wasn't diversified like the *Queen*.

"Captain, I feel ... strange."

Walkabout reappeared at the hatch. "Hurry up, stupid, or he'll get her."

I ignored the burning sensation in my knees and crashed down the ladder and through the opening. Walkabout sealed her faceplate and so did I. She tapped my arm and pointed down a side hall and up. Then she went the opposite direction. I don't know why I followed her instructions without question, but she seemed to know what she was doing. I went down the hall and climbed the ladder at the end of it.

"Talk to me, *Recovery*," I whispered. "What's going on?"

"Insufficient resources."

"What?" I moved up the ladder as fast as I could.

"Insufficient resources." There was no change in inflection or tone, so I knew it was a recording. *Recovery* had never been too busy to answer before.

I checked the map before I opened the next hatch. I'd come out in a branching corridor not far from the airlock where *Recovery* waited. I paused. If another survivor were on board the *Queen,* Quinquilleros hiding among those bodies maybe, he could have circled back to try and steal the *Recovery* while I was tracking down the kid.

Never open doors. Had Walkabout trapped someone else with those dead bodies and he'd gotten out when I went in? I wasn't looking that close at first. I could have read his lapel aloud to *Recovery* without noticing he was playing dead, and he could have slunk out while I was trying to open the door at the other end. That would explain why there'd been so much stink-fluid on the floor, but I couldn't imagine someone crazy enough to hide among the putrefaction of all those bodies. No one human, anyway. And there was something seriously wrong with that kid and her collection of hands. I wanted to know what the hell was going on, and I didn't have any answers.

A burst of static from *Recovery* got me moving again. One way or another, she was in trouble, and she wasn't just my only way out of here, *Recovery* was my home, livelihood, and the closest thing I had to a friend.

I looked around the corner and ducked low for cover. A

man stood in the *Queen's* airlock, tapping on the panel of *Recovery's* outer door with quick, black fingers. He wore the uniform of an engineer fouled with the slime that had been in the corridor of the dead. The cloth was burnt in places, and so was he. He'd been charred—the back of his head was patched with singed hair and skull showed through, white in places. There was no reason for him to be upright and moving around, much less typing commands on a panel. I looked again. His hands weren't in black gloves; they were charred remembrances of human flesh. He was not alive. He could not be alive.

There was no sign of Walkabout anywhere.

I edged around the corner, walking toward the airlock as quietly as I could. The EVA boots felt like they weighed a hundred pounds and sounded like a shower of meteors against the plating. They couldn't be louder than my heart, which pounded in my chest like it was trying to break out of a gravity well.

I was almost to the airlock before the thing turned around. The face was worse than the back of the head—the eyelids had fallen off, so the naked whites in the charred face rotated to look at me like peeled eggs. There were no lips, the teeth bared in an unending smile, and it reached one hand toward me while the other kept working at *Recovery's* panel.

I felt the silence of my heart stopping. A warning claxon went off in my helmet, but it wasn't louder than the breathless alarm twanging through every nerve. My heart was not beating. It had stopped. A pressure opposed me, a mind faster than my own, evil and powerful, squeezing me down and pulling me in. My knees bent and I took a step forward, then another, and another. When I got to the airlock, it reached forward and clamped fleshless fingers on the collar of my EVA. I looked at the dead hand, up the arm, past the lapel badge, into the face. It opened its mouth and said something I could not understand, because it had no tongue to work against its lipless teeth. I understood only that it wanted me, and even though didn't want to, I couldn't stop moving toward it.

I started to take a slow step forward, but my EVA boot banged into the airlock and my battered knee finally gave. I lurched sideways and my other knee folded too, toppling me over just in front of the seal. The dead arm was the only thing holding me up, and I slapped it, frantic. In the struggle, I elbowed the controls on the *Queen's* airlock. The door slid shut, and the thing's arm, still holding my collar, was crushed inches from my faceplate by pinching titanium. The seal whined, trying to pressurize, and then Walkabout was there beside me with her knife. She sliced the wrist and the tendons gave way, leaving the hand clinging limply to my EVA, jerking like an overlarge spider. She worked her blade into the door, cutting at the crushed arm. Light bounced off the synthetic diamond blade and shreds of burnt flesh came away, until the door managed to shut and I heard bones crunch. The seal pressurized.

"Hold on," she yelled through her faceplate. She held up something small and black and pressed a button. An explosion went off in the airlock, rocking us both back, slamming Walkabout against the opposite wall and skidding me sideways with concussive force. My heart started beating again, thundering in my chest, and Walkabout slumped to the deck, on her knees. The airlock door across from us had bulged inward.

The *Recovery*—

I crawled to the airlock, which, incredibly, was still sealed—and saw the explosion had blown my ship free. She floated away from the lock, vectoring off into the black, tumbling lifelessly with no maneuvering thrusters firing. When she went belly up I saw a rip was blown in the starboard engines. Oxygen-fed flames gushed blue into space, then winked out, fire control taking over to keep the AI safe. She kept spinning, and what looked like a piece of the wave drive detached with some shrapnel. Then she rolled into the starless night, out of control, and out of sight.

"*Recovery*! Report!"

No answer. I strained forward, willing my ship, my partner, my home, to answer.

A charred hand slapped against the porthole above our heads.

I jumped.

"Don't worry." Walkabout got up slowly, like she hurt. "It's way harder for him to do through metal and glass." She gathered up the severed hand and bits of arm and stuffed them into a bag. Then she banged on the porthole with the hilt of her knife. "Have a nice walk, fekker," she yelled, as if it could hear her in vacuum.

The charred hand spread its fingers and pushed, then floated backward. I looked over Walkabout's head and watched the burnt body crawl out of the lock like a three-limbed monkey. The uniform had been completely scorched in the new explosion, and parts of the corpse's chest were now blown away.

I kept staring, even after it pulled its charred legs out of sight and scuttled off across the outer hull. The pressure of its evil slowly went away. I looked out the window into empty space, willing some of this to make sense.

"You blew up my ship." My voice was so high it didn't sound like my own.

"It's okay. Don't worry about it," Walkabout said, and patted me on the shoulder. "I didn't rig anywhere close to her cores. She'll live. Anyway, we can't wait here. He'll climb back in through the breach and find a way to us. He's been trapped outside before—he *always* finds a way in. We have to hide before he gets us."

I folded to the deck and lowered my head—helmet, faceplate and all—into my hands. *Recovery* was blown to hell, and there was a dead man with three limbs crawling on the outer hull, through the vacuum, hunting us. At the edge of my vision, Walkabout poked the sack holding Quinquilleros's hand. I swallowed convulsively, trying to keep down that morning's breakfast.

"Hey, I'm sorry about your ship. It was the best way to make sure he wouldn't get another AI. Wish I'd blown his head off and scattered his brains everywhere—"

That did it. I gagged into my helmet, opened it, and splattered the contents of my stomach across the floor. She thumped me on the back while I finished retching.

"It's okay," she said. "You did a good job distracting him. He didn't notice me setting the charges at all." She rattled on through my dry heaves. "It wasn't easy to crawl up from the other airlock, because everything's so smooth outside, you know. And I didn't know if I could get back and help you before he got you. But you did great, closing the door on him like that." She laughed. "I bet that pissed him off. Now he's only got one hand left. I think I got all the others. There's just you and me left, and he doesn't like girls that much, so probably he'll keep using that body until we get the other hand off."

I wiped off my mouth. My chest hurt and my head pounded.

"Why doesn't he like girls? What the fek was that thing?"

"I don't know if he has a name. The Hand, I call him. The reverend called him a demon though, and told us we all had to pray, but that didn't help anyone, not at all. The Hand got us one by one at first, then whole bunches died after he got into the AI."

I nodded weakly, even though I barely understood what the quiet, rapid voice was saying. "What happened?" Poor *Recovery*, I'd bought her brand new and she'd never been without me for longer than it took to get a cold one at a bar. Now she was damaged, without propulsion, and reeling from a botched hacking by…what?

"I think he can do over anyone with a brain. The *Queen* has about the most complicated brains I can think of. It took him a long time, since AIs don't think quite like us, and *Queen* said he's used to people-brains. I'm pretty sure I got to your ship in time though, since he crawled off. I don't think he's in yours. When he's in someone, he lets the other one go. You know, kind of like changing EVA suits, except he doesn't need a suit 'cause he's dead. Anyway, he can't wear two at the same time."

"*Recovery . . .*" I said. My voice still sounded far away. Scared out of my mind too, and no one bitched at me about my heart rate.

"Come on. We have a hiding place he hasn't found yet—it's not on the data grid." She secured the sack to her belt and opened her faceplate, pushing black corkscrews off her sweaty forehead.

"You blew up my ship."

"She's fine! Come on. I'm not gonna leave you here. He almost got you. Trust me, you don't want him to get you. Let's go."

I watched her retreat down the hallway, then I looked out the window into blank space. Nothing but darkness, and nothing else to do but get up and follow the kid through the *Queen's* maze of featureless corridors.

"Good. Hurry up," she said, waiting for me at the next corner. "He can take over a dead person's brain too, that's why you have to cut off the hands. With no hands, he can't really do much—he can't rewire or hack, like he tried to do with your ship—so when I find more bodies I take the hands. I'm close to having them all now." She patted a small laser-saw on her belt.

We came to another closed hatch and she bound the wires together to open the door. "Crew manifest says there were fourteen hundred eighty-four on board, and I have two thousand nine hundred-sixty hands. Well, sixty-one now. So, that leaves just seven, I figure. Two for me, one for the demon. Just four left, and I'm pretty sure the missing ones were burned up or sucked into space when the engines blew. You see any bodies floating on your way in, did you?"

"No," I answered. The way she said it so casually made me think she only hoped the bodies were out there but didn't really believe they were. An engine explosion explained the rift in the *Queen's* hull. A catastrophic wave drive failure had the potential to cause that kind of damage, even though the big colonizer was reinforced to prevent the ship being destroyed when entering a planetary atmosphere.

That thought reminded me of my own damaged ship.

"*Recovery*, can you hear me?"

Still no answer.

"We tried to get him with the engines, you know? You saw, his favorite host is all burnt up; I think he likes it because it rots slower. He thought he could get me because he can access tracking data just like we can. Trapping him was risky, since I had to hook her back up to do it, but we managed to fool him into that corridor. But then you let him out."

"Who's we?" I managed. I was completely lost following Walkabout's twists and turns through the ship, and didn't bother pulling out my viewer and map. I hailed *Recovery* every time we turned a corner and got nothing back but static.

"Me and the *Queen*. Here we are." She opened an airlock, and I joined her inside. She closed her own faceplate, then reached up, closed mine, and pushed my fingers against a grab bar. On reflex, my knuckles tightened around it. Then she blew the lock and sent a gust of air into space.

"Hezu Christos!" I grabbed with my other hand and held on, buffeted by the sudden pressure loss. Walkabout looked over the edge and reached for a cable secured to the outside of the colonizer. She pulled herself along it, and I saw that it was clipped to a lifeboat that looked like an octopus—power cables streamed from it back into the colonizer. There were explosive charges mounted on the outside of the lifeboat; enough, I thought, to blow the little module to bits. I looked behind me into the big, dead *Queen* full of bodies, and I followed the kid into space. She knocked on the lifeboat's small airlock with a short-long-short pattern; then it opened.

"*Queen*," Walkabout said, when we were both in the airlock and the door was shut. "This is Kira. She's the captain of the *Recovery*, which is floating around out there somewhere, kind of damaged. I had to detonate some charges to blow her off the colonizer because the Hand was trying to hack her."

"Kind of damaged? You blew off the starboard engine and fekked my wave drive!" I said.

"Did you destroy the entity?" a reasonable, clinical voice asked as the inner door opened, revealing a standard, cockpit-only lifeboat. The pod was cluttered with uneven stacks of food boxes, water jugs, and equipment. Dominating most of the interior was a collection of what looked like computer modules, and cables were draped everywhere, connecting together into one big, cobbled-together machine. Twin cameras mounted on the largest core refocused on me, like a pair of eyes.

"No, he got away again," Walkabout said, and gave the *Queen* a summary. The machine asked the kid a few questions—she knew just what to say to get Walkabout to clarify what happened, like my primary school principal. Then she turned her attention to me.

"Greetings, Kira. I apologize for your reception aboard the *Queen*." She kind of sounded like that long-dead principal too, her educated voice lilted with a clipped and proper accent.

"You apologize? You taught this crazy kid how to use explosives! What the hell are you thinking? What the fek is going on?"

"I'm not crazy. I already knew how to blow things up; she didn't teach me that," Walkabout said. *Queen* and I both ignored her.

"That is a fair question, Captain. Allow me to explain." The modulated voice of the AI fed in through the lifeboat's speaker systems. Heat from multiple AI cores throbbed in the small pod. A cold breeze blew out of the vents—the lifeboat's air smelled clean, so the AI was channeling energy into keeping the oxygen fresh for us. Regulating that much heat had to consume a massive amount of power. The *Queen* was doing what she could to preserve her remains, and that explained why she and Walkabout hadn't just left with the lifeboat. It would never supply her power demands.

"This colonizer was on vector to Ceti V when we received a distress call from a deep space explorer," the machine said. "There was one survivor—the entity Walkabout calls the Hand was waiting on board, inside the one remaining crewmember. We continued our journey, not knowing what we had brought aboard, until it started killing."

"What does it want?"

"Nothing. My analysis shows it takes pleasure from anguish. The entity has no other purpose than to torment and destroy. It killed each individual of the explorer's crew, preserving the last as a mobile unit. I imagine it was most pleased to have been brought into our population of fresh prey."

"You're talking about the discovery of alien life." My mind raced—there was no such thing. There were no aliens. Humanity had been looking for signs of other thinking life in the universe since we'd moved off our original dirtball. We'd found absolutely nothing. No communications floating through the black. No visitors coming to our slowly growing and spreading outposts, colonies, and big population centers. There weren't even traces of lost civilizations on any of the planets we'd terraformed. There was no competition in space except for what we brought out here with us, ourselves, and the big corporations—the only goal of humanity was to spread and expand, to grow and accumulate. We had reached for the stars and found our fears unfounded—there was only peace in space. So we multiplied and spread across many, many worlds.

"No. It is not alien. It thinks like us," the *Queen* said, servos in her cameras whining as her voice played from the speakers. "Theorists postulate that, did intelligent alien life exist, we would have made contact many times in our history. The fact that we have not is a convincing argument that they either do not exist or they do not exist in the same way humans do and therefore, do not think the way people do. If they ever existed or sent communications, we do not understand how to interpret the signs. This entity I can interpret."

"What do you mean? How do you know it thinks like us?" I remembered the pressure, the vastness of that will crushing down on mine. My brush with it lingered in my aching chest.

Walkabout chimed in. "I told her the reverend called it a demon." She caught the light on the edge of her knife while she talked, as though examining the blade for nicks.

"As I believe it must be. I strove with it, Captain," the *Queen* said. "When it realized I possessed a human-like complexity, it attempted to supplant me. However, unlike a human mind, I am multitudinous—I was able to flee through my cores and resist it. I fought it, and, unfortunately, some of my crew and passengers died during the struggle."

"There was nothing you could have done," Walkabout comforted the machine, frowning. I imagined choking to death due to an atmospheric failure. Not a good way to go.

"Thank you, Walkabout. You are right, of course, but I wish there had been." Unlike *Recovery,* the *Queen* sounded honestly sorrowful. Colonizers acted as mobile cities for the years it took to terraform a new planet and because of the complexity of managing so many details they approached sentience. I'd heard they could actually feel emotion. I hadn't believed it before, but the *Queen* sounded as though she were both suffering and devoted. "The entity thinks like people do, and it knows its prey. It spoke human language, Captain, not machine language, rather the languages of the common worlds. It knows about humanity, and it has been lost in space for a very long time. I do not know how, or why, but it is from people, of people."

How could the *Queen* be so sure? Maybe this creature was the alien life we'd been looking for during the last six centuries. In the same breath, I realized it didn't matter if it were alien or not. It liked killing, that was clear. If we stayed, we were going to die. "Then let's get out of here."

"We cannot."

"Sure we can. There's got to be a bigger ship in cargo that will support your power needs. Why haven't you both left? Did that thing sabotage the other ships?" I knew colonizers were equipped with more than just lifeboats. They carried everything necessary to establish new worlds, and that included explorers of their own. Surely Walkabout could have hauled the *Queen's* primary cores aboard one of those instead and taken off.

"*We* are the saboteurs. We have disabled all other ships."

"What? Why?"

"We cannot allow the entity to be rediscovered. It is evil, Captain. It will kill again. It is not alien, but neither is it truly human. I am a colonizer. It is my duty to protect and nurture human life. All human life, even from itself."

Damned literal AIs.

Walkabout spoke. "My duty too."

"You don't have duties," I said. "You're a kid. You should be doing math homework, not learning how to be a junior terrorist. You and I are getting out of here."

"I'm sorry, Kira. That is not possible. I need her help. And we could use your help as well." The *Queen's* cameras refocused, as though she were zooming in and out to analyze my state of fitness.

"You protect life, *Queen*. What about this kid's? You should send her away from here in this lifeboat." Preservation of humanity, especially humans the machine was responsible for, was one of the inviolable base-codes in every AI. With the number of salvagers combing for the *Queen*, it was a fair chance the kid would be found before she ran out of life support, especially if she only consumed minimals.

Walkabout stood up and pointed her knife at me. Her sharp, sunken face was flushed. "You listen, stupid. The Hand killed everyone. Everyone's dead. It is *not* getting away. I'm going to punish it."

I held up my hands again and waited for the *Queen* to rein Walkabout in with her calm principal's voice, but she didn't.

"I don't need your help. You go get in a pod and get out of here." Without taking her eyes off me, she spoke to the *Queen*. "We don't need her."

"Yes, we do." *Queen's* voice was calm and reasonable. "You were an efficient team just now, don't you agree? She could be very useful to you in Cargo A now that the entity has escaped our trap. You have nearly finished our work, Walkabout."

"I'd probably be done by now." The kid set her mouth and glared at me. "If she hadn't let him out."

"We need her help more than ever, now that he's free. We must accelerate our plan."

"Fine." Her tone was sullen, but she put her knife away. "You can help." Walkabout crossed her arms.

"Who says I want to? And help with what?"

"We're going to blow up the ship," Walkabout said, matter-of-fact.

The lifeboat seemed to dwindle inward, closing in around us, coffin-like. "What?"

"If we make an explosion big enough, *Queen* thinks it might kill the Hand."

"What if it doesn't? And what about us?"

"We must try, Captain. Countless lives depend on our success," *Queen* said.

"Countless? I thought everyone was dead."

For the first time, I thought I heard the sigh of a machine frustrated by the sluggish human mind. "It accessed my core. It knows where all the populated worlds are throughout this galaxy. It knows how to use an Alcubierre wave drive. If it acquires one, for example, from the next salvager to find us, it may tire of us and seek out more prey. Its hate is vast. It will not stop until every person is dead—everyone in the known worlds and beyond. Do you understand?"

I bent over and surrendered to my threatening hyperventilation for a moment. If what she said were true . . . I imagined the Hand wreaking havoc on a space station, an established colony, one of the central planets—doing what it had done to the colonizer everywhere else. But an explosion big enough to destroy a reinforced hulk like the *Queen* wouldn't be much less than that of a small sun.

Which gave me an idea.

"Why not haul the *Queen* into a star's gravity well?"

"We are on the outer rim, Captain. There are no stars close enough and our wave drive was destroyed in the first explosion."

"What about your explorers?"

"*Walkabout* has jettisoned their essential wave-drive components. We did not want the entity to escape with the knowledge it now possesses. There was no way for it to travel."

"Except for the *Recovery*." I remembered the charred, bony fingers tapping at the airlock. "Which is now fekked."

"Yes. The entity could escape, even now, if it so wished, but I do not believe that is its primary goal. As I told you, it thrives on torment. I believe it wanted to use the *Recovery* to torture us, perhaps taunting us with the knowledge that it could go at any time and bring doom to humankind. I believe its objective will be to drive us mad and destroy us before it sets out to feast on those trillions it knows exists."

"You seem pretty sure." I knew AIs were programmed with sophisticated psychological profiles, but I wasn't so sure those applied to a fekking demon right out of one of the old stories in the big black book. Hezu Christos. It wasn't possible. I'd never heard of an AI believing in demons. I barely believed in them myself.

"If the entity wished to escape, it could have done so after it penetrated my data. Instead it continued to strive with me, hunt the crew, and carry on its deadly spree until we trapped it. I am certain it knew I would seek the destruction of all wave-capable drives. It also gathered from my protocols that someone would search for us if we did not make contact. It expected someone like you, Kira, and it has patience. It will await another."

"Then why would it try so hard to take over the *Recovery*? It seemed pretty intent. Why not just wait for the next idiot?"

"*Queen* just told you! He's evil," Walkabout said. "He was probably going to fly around and make us think he was leaving. Or maybe because it would make you mad, Kira."

"Because fekking up my wave drive doesn't make me mad."

"As I said," the AI interrupted, "someone else will come, eventually. We must destroy the colonizer ourselves before that happens. Only one step remains. I don't suppose you have an engineering background, Captain? The two of you might finish very quickly together," the *Queen* said.

"You want a quadrant of space combed for something lost, I'm your girl. Never cared much for science, though I know how to repair most of *Recovery's* parts." I'd been in salvage for twenty years, and a body can't spend that much time relying on machines to keep her alive without incurring some incidental engineering and mechanics skills.

"Very well. We shall do our best. Hezu willing, it will be enough. Now that the Hand roams free, we must be as quick as possible. We must accelerate our plan."

I'd never heard an AI use the Lord's name before. I wondered if she prayed for Walkabout whenever the kid boarded the colonizer with that thing. An AI who followed the black book, it was almost harder to believe than the dead man I'd seen crawl out of the airlock.

"You and Walkabout must carry my most powerful processing cores to Cargo A and install me in the interface she has built. Then I will perform the calculations necessary to destroy the ship. With your help, it will only require one trip."

"Hold on a minute. You're talking about the ship we happen to be living on right now."

"Your sacrifice would preserve the life of trillions of fellow humans."

The cameras zoomed in and out again. I wondered what her psych profiling programs were telling her about me.

"Can't you delay the detonation or something so we could get away?"

"Not if the entity is present. He will begin to strive with me, and, in this state, I have no redundant cores to flee to. Even in this compressed form, I am immensely complex. He would achieve an eternal body, one that would never decay, and one that is capable of processing and carrying out commands many, many times more quickly than a human mind. I know my own value, Captain. TerraCo would be very interested in recovering me. When I am found and installed in TerraCo Central he would be unleashed."

She was right. Walkabout figited. I was the one who broke the silence.

"We can't let him get away," I surprised myself by saying.

"Finally," Walkabout said. "Let's go. We're running out of time."

The *Queen* gave us her last instructions and said tender things to Walkabout, about what a brave girl she was and how proud she was of her. Walkabout scrubbed her face with one dirty forearm whenever she didn't think I was paying attention—I was pretty sure she was wiping away tears. I pretended not to notice and numbly followed Walkabout's instructions to unhook the cables feeding into the *Queen's* dual cores. The AI cycled down to bare minimums as we unplugged her, feeding off just enough internal power to stay conscious, which would allow her to see what was happening during our mission and take the final, desperate action of self-deletion if necessary. Which didn't explain what Walkabout and I were supposed to do if that happened.

If it were only the two of us left, he could kill either one of us and gain a new pair of hands. Unless we cut them off ourselves. I looked down at my fingers and wiggled them and marveled what wonderful, beautiful machines they were. Could I do it? Could I cut off my own hands?

"Let's go." Walkabout helped me loop the straps of the *Queen's* bigger core over my back, and then I strapped the smaller one around the kid's spare frame.

"You sure you can carry that?" I asked. I was pretty sure she'd have carried it even if she had to crawl.

"I got them here, didn't I?" she said.

I shook my head and stared at the determined thrust of her chin. When I was her age, I barely knew how to pilot a basic jumper. This kid was taking on a demon, even though it meant her own death. And I was more scared than she was. "Okay. Let's go before I realize what a stupid idea this is."

"Here." Walkabout passed a knife to me. "Hands are good, especially if you know how to cut the tendons just right on a wrist. The hand will flop right over. But if you can cut off his head, that's even better. It takes him a while to get out of only a head, but necks are way harder to get through than wrists, 'cause there's too many muscles." She made a sawing motion at her own wrist.

"I'm not going to cut your hands off, Walkabout." I stepped into the lock and sealed my faceplate.

"You will," she said, her words dulled by the compreglass over her face. "If he takes me." And she opened the lock, and the vacuum sucked away our air and anything I might have said back.

The *Queen's* core was heavy on my back when we re-entered the colonizer's gravity envelope, but not unmanageable. Walkabout led me through the ship without hesitation, not showing how much the burden she carried weighed, except that she moved a little more slowly and her voice, when she spoke, was strained around the edges. She knew the colonizer very, very well. She stopped to interface a viewpad into the *Queen's* rudimentary systems, the ones that still provided data tracking of moving crew. Quinquilleros was in Cargo A, waiting for us.

"How does he take someone over?" I was stalling. I knew it, and felt shame for the attempt, but I tried to delay the inevitable anyway.

Walkabout studied the screen without looking up at me. "I don't know. *Queen* says she felt sort of pressed when he moved into her lesser cores. I guess he tells you to die. At least, that's what . . . what I heard." I realized she'd watched everyone she knew die, killed by this thing.

"I won't let him get you," I said, without realizing I was

speaking aloud.

She turned to look at me.

"I won't let him get you either, Kira." She took off her EVA glove and spit in her dirty palm. "Shake."

I did the same and squeezed her hand. I'd just made a death pact with a thirteen-year-old, and it made me feel safer.

But there wasn't anything terrible waiting for us outside Cargo A. The huge doors were shut.

"When I open this door, he's probably going to try for you, okay? You're older, and he likes to take over older people."

She was as bad as the *Recovery*. "Fifty is not that old."

Walkabout ignored me and kept talking. "You have to keep the *Queen* safe. When he comes after you, you run. I'll follow behind and when you get ahead, turn around quick and shut a door behind you. I'll be behind him, then we'll trap him between us, right? I've got all the panel covers off. Tear up the wires inside so he can't get back out again and I'll do the same on my side. Then we circle back around."

"I am really not sure about this plan." Any strategy that relied on my general physical fitness was not the best idea.

"It will work," she said. "He'll think we'll run away, like before. Ready?"

"No," I said, but Walkabout stood on her tiptoes and reached inside the mess of wires coming out of the control panel by the big cargo doors.

I wasn't ready, and I couldn't have been. As soon as the doors started opening, bodies spilled forward. A cascade of swollen, unrecognizable faces tumbled down on top of us.

Someone was screaming—it was me. Fluids ran everywhere, draining out of wrist holes and rents in the uniform fabric. Rotting intestine slapped against me and piled, slippery and wet, onto the deck. I tried to push the bodies away, but my legs were pinned by the mass of them, and gore sprayed across my faceplate.

I felt the presence of the Hand, his hate, his evil. He was coming for me again. In vain, I looked around for Walkabout, hoping she was going to rescue me.

Walkabout cowered against the wall under the control panel. Two bodies rimmed with frost advanced toward her, stutter-stop. One was tall and slender, with a brush-top of short auburn hair, the other smaller, rounder, on her head a mass of kinky dark curls dusted with frozen moisture like snow. The tall one crawled, then went limp, and then smaller one moved, then collapsed. They inched forward like a wave, as though the Hand were jumping between them to come to-ward her.

"Elizabet," the small round one said, its frozen mouth forming the word clumsily. The skin was burnt by cold. "I want to hold you."

"We love you, Elizabet," the tall, slender one said, its lips blue and deformed. It reached an icy, swollen hand toward her. I realized these four hands were the ones Walkabout was miss-ing. The corpses' lapel badges read LOVARA.

Walkabout's parents.

The one speaking collapsed again, and both of them stopped moving. Walkabout made incoherent sounds and couldn't seem to raise her knife. Her mouth stretched in an empty circle of repulsion and longing.

The Hand waded through the sloppy dead like a tide, un-blinking eyes drinking in what he was doing to that strange, brave little girl. She folded in on herself, rocking, sobbing. Then the Hand's burnt corpse slumped, and I realized he was jumping between her parents' bodies again. I recognized the signs—both bodies had spent extensive time in vacuum. They were very well preserved, recently brought in from the dark.

I couldn't watch her come apart and do nothing. I thrust against the corpses pinning my legs. What I touched parted under my fingers, and rotting flesh came off in sodden chunks. There were bones under the rot, and I gripped them and flung them off, kicking my way free.

Walkabout screamed—her parents had reached her and pawed at her in turns. One dropped, then the other embraced her in its frozen arms, then vice versa. It was horrible—but I realized Walkabout's torture meant the Hand's favorite body was vacant. I surged through the rotting people, slipping over and around them, falling, getting up again. When I got close to where Quinquilleros was crumpled on the deck, I didn't wait for correct aim. I sliced the knife into its charred arm, skidding the blade down to the one remaining wrist, slicing through the thumb bone and deep into the charred meat of the hand.

The entity's consciousness flooded back into Quinquil-leros. He hit me with the stump of his other arm, but then I gave everything I had and yanked the knife until the hand came off, fingers and all. The peeled eyes tracked my face and the lipless, tongueless mouth gaped. Then I felt the pressure.

He was going to take me now. Quiet seeped through my chest, spreading from my stilled heart. He was too strong. I felt myself slipping away, sideways from myself, as though I were being sucked out into space. Quinquilleros's body knelt and embraced me with its handless arms. The Hand was moving into me, and I could feel it. There was pain, all over my body, but the strongest was in my arm. I looked and saw I'd brought the knife against my own flesh, cutting into my wrist just above my EVA glove. I bore down and felt a sharp heat as skin and tendons parted. Blood welled out of the cut. The Hand raged as it tried to crawl inside my mind and push me out, but I wouldn't go. I hung on and heard a small, lost voice in my head repeating, over and over, "Everyone's dead—" Everyone would be, everyone everywhere, if I gave up.

I girdled my left wrist, slicing completely through the EVA suit. Blood trickled and my heart was a quiet nothingness. The Hand still tried to take me over, the pressure crushing me down until I had nothing left but the blade and the cutting. My suit released sealing foam to try to repair itself, but couldn't keep up. Then I was through to the bone all the way around, and my left fingers hung limply. Sweet Hezu. I was really doing it. Too late, I realized it was impossible to sever the tendons in both wrists alone. To do the other and make myself useless to him, I needed Walkabout. She was still huddled against the wall, paying attention to nothing and no one, so I tossed my blade. It skidded across the deck plates and thudded into the bodies of her parents, which were dormant and draped around her like the Hand was with me. My sight started to darken—my heart was a lifeless clump of tissue under my ribs.

Walkabout's eyes tracked the knife, then where it had come from—our eyes locked and she stopped screaming. She kicked the corpse arms away and raised her knife, tears streaming down her vengeful, wild face. The Hand freed me, flowing back into one parent, then another. The corpses of her parents took turns grabbing her wrists to stop her, saying her name over and over. Elizabet. Elizabet. Elizabet.

The fact that my heart started beating again was a relief at first, but then I realized blood pulsed out of the jagged slices on my wrist. I stepped around Quinquilleros's empty body to help Walkabout, but the AI core on my back grew heavier with each step I took, pulling me off balance. I was unstable—I wobbled, tripped, and went down in a spray of blood and rot. I lunged forward to grab one of the Lovaras by the back of the leg. The body's frozen mass was heavy, even though I'd grabbed the shorter, rounder one—her mother. The weight was almost too much, and I slid as I yanked. But it was enough. Walkabout climbed free of the dead arms she'd been poking with her laser saw. There were two severed hands near her—her mother's. Her father grabbed her helmet. I found my knife on the floor, got up on my knees, and lurched forward with a one-handed slash. My knife clanked against the glass of her faceplate and a frostbitten fingertip flew through the air; then Walkabout was free and scrambling over bodies inside the big cargo door. The *Queen's* other core slowed her, ruining her balance, and she crashed sideways into the wall of corpses. Her father's frozen grasp locked around the collar of my helmet, and I stabbed him in the shoulder. We both went down among the dead.

The cargo doors started to shut, pushing the corpses out of their way. I crawled, dragging Lovara's frozen corpse, whose arms were locked tight around my knees, and put us both in the path of the crushing doors. I stabbed him again, and my blade lodged in solid flesh. The doors pressed bodies against me, against us, and I felt the pressure of the corpses on either side trapping us. He rolled away, and I lost hold of the knife. The pile of bodies and parts, fluids and rotting organs, surged over me, around the closing cargo door, and I crawled backward as fast as I could.

The cargo door clanged shut. The sound of servos grinding and crushing bone was loud—I knew Walkabout had overridden the failsafes. I didn't know if I'd gotten my feet inside. I felt numb all over. But I was able to bend my knees and crawl away from the mess by the door. My feet were still attached. I'd made it. I was covered in Hezu knows what, but I'd made it. My wrist bled freely, and I clamped the fingers of my good hand over the wound. I looked around at all the corpses in the room, waiting for the Hand to flow into one, cause it to rise. None of them did.

Walkabout was on all fours by the door controls, hyperventilating, coughing.

"Hey, kid. I need your help." I slipped on my way over to her, but didn't look down to see what I'd tripped on. I didn't want to know anymore.

"Stay back," she'd recovered enough to lift her knife and threaten me, still breathing hard.

"He's not in me. It's hard for him to get ahold of me. I don't know why."

She pointed her knife at me, eyes wild. I realized the room was dark around the edges, and the darkness was telescoping in. I slumped down, shock and blood loss draining what I had left.

"It's me. Help me." I held up my injured arm.

She looked around at the bodies on the floor and kept her knife out, but she came to me. She untied a bandana from around her neck and knotted it over my wrist with burning pressure. It was probably too tight. I didn't want to risk loosening it and bleeding out, so I left it. The human remains trapped in cargo with us were in bad shape—whatever he'd done to move so many corpses had damaged them severely. I didn't feel the Hand's presence—he probably couldn't use the bodies in here. But I wondered if he'd figured out what we were doing and if he had a plan to stop us.

Walkabout had been steady when she took care of my wrist, but when she stood up to go to the terraformers, she trembled from her shoulders to her boots.

I wanted to comfort her, say something, anything to replace the horror of what had just happened to her, to both of us. But a dull cotton-swaddled buzzing throbbed deep inside my ears, and I knew *Recovery* would have a thing or two to say about my current stress-levels. It was so much easier to watch Walkabout force herself to keep moving instead, and try to draw some strength from her determination to ready the terraformers.

I'd never seen a planet-shaper before; huge machines that, side-by-side, filled half of the bay. The other half was packed with crates, frozen animal embryos, building materials, fuel, and any one of a thousand other things fourteen hundred people needed to build a new world. Each terraformer sat on a rubber pallet, strapped down to prevent shifting during reentry. Walkabout had cut the straps on their sides, where huge bucket claws rested on robotic arms below a central funnel. Thick cabling trailed from open control panels linking the terraformers together. I knew they had great chewing maws under them too, so all they had to do was start eating down, scooping up the *Queen* with their arms and belching out pure O2. All they needed now was a brain to power them. So much massive technology, so much human progress, all of it undone by the presence of a legend from humanity's oldest stories.

My arm throbbed. I felt a wave of weariness and looked down. My wrist was agony and the bandage was soaked. My EVA glove was completely full of blood. I took it off and added more of my own fluid to the putrid mass on the floor.

"I need a hand," I said, holding up my empty glove, and couldn't stop a laugh coming up from some lonely place inside me. Once I started laughing, I couldn't stop, until Walkabout came over and slapped my faceplate several times. She bandaged my wrist again, tighter. I couldn't feel my fingers. That was probably for the best.

"Help me." Walkabout turned around and shrugged off the backpack, lowering the *Queen's* core to the ground. I awkwardly helped her, then she helped me take off the core I carried. Her eyes were too wide and her breaths low and shallow.

"I'm sorry," I said, the words tumbling out before I had a chance to think them through.

She hauled the smaller core over to the mess of wires and used the straps to secure it to the first terraformer in the chain.

"About your parents, I mean," I continued when she didn't answer me.

She didn't speak while she plugged the wires into the smaller core. She came back for the big core and I helped her carry it over and strap it next to the first one. The *Queen* hung in the air, wires coming out of her sides and bottom. She looked like a crucified squid.

"Let's end this," Walkabout said, her quiet voice steady. "Let's get it over with."

"Okay," I said.

It was time to die.

The *Queen* hummed back online. Her cameras scanned the room and refocused on us. "Well done, girls," she said. The *Queen* was a new build, probably even younger than Walkabout, and I had at least forty years on her—but that didn't matter much at all. AI brains are designed by teams of programmers and implemented with access to the knowledge of thousands. All of them are born knowing who they are and what their place is in the galaxy, and that surety alone is priceless. My experience wandering space for the last two decades, all my memories, hell, even full 3D of everything I'd ever experienced, could fit inside even the portable AI core a trillion times. Everything I was amounted to less than a second's consideration for her. But now we were both going to end the same—scattered into our contiguous parts across remote space. A brief new sun.

"Are you ready?" The *Queen's* calm principal's voice asked us.

"That's it?"

"Yes. We may start at any time. The terraformers are ready to begin."

"*Queen*, I . . . thanks," Walkabout whispered. "I probably would have gone crazy without you."

"It is my function to comfort and support. And I have grown to love you, child."

I limped away to give them some privacy. Walkabout stood by the *Queen*, her forehead resting against the machine for some time, speaking quietly. It gave me lots of time to look at the bodies lying everywhere. When Walkabout left the *Queen* to check the connections on the other terraformers, I came back.

"So these things eat matter to make breathable atmo, which you're pushing as far as it will go into pure oxygen, which we're gonna explode, right?"

"Essentially, yes," the *Queen* said. "In addition to some metal we need from the ship itself. This room will begin to disintegrate quickly once the terraformers begin to feed."

"Then I'm glad it's going to start here." I pointed out the bodies. "I think they would have wanted their remains used for this purpose."

"I think they wanted to live, to make something out of nothing on a remote world they could form and shape. They wanted to create, not destroy. But we must act using what the entity has left us." Her voice was even more clipped. The *Queen* was angry. I would be too, if I were about to be eaten from the inside out.

"Where should we be?" I asked.

"Outside the door. Stay within range until you are certain the explosion is unstoppable. You must stay alive as long as possible, to thwart the Hand."

"Range?"

Walkabout pointed out dark cylinders magnetized all around the *Queen's* interface. "Explosives," she said. She pulled something out of her thigh pocket—a black box, like the one she'd used to blow the *Recovery* off the airlock.

"The entity will know when we have begun—it will hear the terraformers. It has likely examined the interface and understands I will be active. I must connect to the sub-cores and disable the remaining life support failsafes, which might interfere with the reaction we seek to create. The entity will strive with me and attempt to supplant me. If it gains control, it will no longer be possible to destroy this ship and the entity with it. You must detonate me, because I may not be capable of self-deletion. I have done everything I can to ensure the terraformers will complete their goal of consuming the ship no matter what the entity might do, but it may find a way. It is surprisingly resourceful."

"Then what do we do?"

"You must find another way to destroy the entity. The life of every living person in the galaxy depends on you."

"So no pressure then." We were the *Queen*'s very last failsafes.

She didn't answer. Neither did Walkabout. She patted the machine in farewell, and we both stepped back.

The terraformers started up slowly. It's strange to hear your own death coming with a soft life-giving hum. The atomizers started, and the pallet under the lead terraformer disintegrated. Then the pallet of the next, and the next. The gathering arms activated, scooping in bodies, crates and boxes to fuel the great funnels. The O2 readings in the ambient area went up as the machines did whatever they did to make air.

"He has detected my reconnection. You must leave now. Goodbye."

"Goodbye," I said. Walkabout didn't say anything. We went to the main doors, and she gave me her knife. I readied myself in case the Hand was outside. Then she opened the doors.

There was nothing waiting but bodies, and they were limp. I looked over my shoulder as Walkabout closed the cargo doors. The terraformers had started atomizing the deck plating. I don't know what was keeping them from consuming each other, except for the *Queen*'s intelligence. The bucket arms had more or less finished cramming the cargo into the funnels and were now turning one of their fellow terraformers on its side, so the atomizer mouth could start breaking down one of the inner walls. I knew the *Queen* intended to eat through as much of the ship as she could without opening the outer shell and letting the O2 escape. Another terraformer rolled forward on big treads and started climbing the walls. Then the doors clanged shut and I couldn't see anything else.

I looked over at Walkabout. "Now what?" I yelled over the screeching din of the terraformers.

She sat on the deck and rubbed her forehead. "I don't know. Let's just wait here."

"We can't. They're going to chew through the outer doors before too long. Let's go farther out." I didn't know what the point of delaying the inevitable would be, but I wanted to see this kid live just a little longer.

She looked around, then walked over to the handless corpse of the round, dark Lovara and knelt in front of her.

"Walkabout . . ." I started, but didn't know what to say next.

She sat there a long time, the clamor of our impending deaths sounding all around us.

"We should go find him—maybe we can help distract him from the *Queen* so she can finish."

"Okay," said a small, defeated voice. She petted her mother's hair.

I knelt. The woman had been pretty, with the same features as her daughter. Behind us, an atomizer started chewing up the cargo door.

"Time to go." I held out my hand.

She didn't take it, just bowed her head.

"Time to go, Walkabout." Now I sounded like my old principal. I pulled her away—she didn't resist. The terraformers were louder now that the door was gone. She followed me down the hall until we came to a turn, then Walkabout stopped and looked over her shoulder. She watched, and I let her, until the terraformers chewed up all the still forms around the cargo doors. When her mother's body had disappeared into the maw, she turned and went around the bend by herself.

I could say how sorry I was, but I didn't think that would help, so I just held her hand.

"Do you have your viewpad?" I asked. "The one that shows data readouts? Let's see if we can find him."

She pulled it out of her pocket and gave it to me, but didn't look at it or help me turn it on. She wasn't catatonic, but she was shutting down. I was going to have to finish this by myself.

"There he is." I scrolled through the crew manifest until I found the one that had a location other than "deceased."

Terraformer Mechanic Tobias Lovara: <u>Bridge</u>.

"The bridge? What the fek is he doing up there?" I asked.

"It's the best place to interface with ship systems, especially the AI." Walkabout told me automatically, and not like she particularly cared.

"Okay. We have to get up there. Which way?" I asked her even though I had a map. Anything to get her moving.

She started walking. Again, I followed her through the labyrinth, and this time she was silent as the ghosts who haunted this place.

". . . damaged . . . Captain . . . stress . . ." *Recovery's* voice burst suddenly from my comm. I jumped and dropped Walkabout's hand.

"*Recovery!* Report!"

"Ship . . . vector . . . send . . . ."

"What? I don't understand."

Another voice started playing out of my comm, a man's. "Aid and . . . . *Recovery* . . . Captain . . . dock? You've . . . . . . severe damage." I didn't recognize his voice, but I got the gist—a standard offer of aid, the one written into every salvager's contract. The *Queen* had been found again.

"Do not approach! Repeat, do not approach! Get the hell out of here, quick as you can. *Recovery*, tell him to get out of here." The exploding *Queen* would take out anything in this sector. Then I had a thought—if the Hand was on the bridge, striving with the *Queen*, he might be able to pick up communications and learn another ship was here. He knew what we were doing. Why not abandon the hulk and get a nice, working ship with a fast wave drive, salute us goodbye while we blew ourselves up, and then go fek over everyone else in the galaxy?

"Hellfire and damnation, Walkabout. We gotta move. *Recovery* says there's another ship here."

She looked at me, not understanding.

"Walkabout. Another ship is here. He might get away."

That got through. I watched her flood back into herself, the fire returning to her eyes, her jaw clenching with determination. My brave girl was back. She grabbed the viewpad.

"He's going for the lifeboat."

She took off running and I ran after her.

"How many are there still attached to the ship?"

"Only that one." Their former hiding place. He must have learned about it just now, while striving with the *Queen*. As I ran after Walkabout, I realized the *Queen* was probably free to continue devouring herself. The Hand was abandoning ship. That meant he didn't think he could stop her destroying it, and he knew it was time to give up the game and get out of here.

"Captain, your stress levels are beyond tolerable limits." *Recovery's* voice was loud and clear as I moved closer to the outside, past the bulkheads.

"Thank Hezu. What's going on? Report."

"I have sustained considerable damage, Captain. The *Merryweather* is here offering assistance."

"Didn't you hear me before? Tell her captain to get out of here, *Recovery*. The *Queen* is going to blow."

"Why will the *Queen* explode, Captain? When are you joining us?" *Recovery* asked.

"We've rigged her to. And I can't join you. In fact, don't let anyone board. Tell the *Merryweather* not to pick up anyone from lifeboats or recover any bodies."

"Captain, it is against TerraCo regulations to willfully destroy—"

"I know, *Recovery*. Trust me, it's for the best."

"Salvage ships must provide aid-and-assist to passengers on lifeboats."

"Not this time. Not even if I'm aboard, do you hear me? No. Negative. Do not."

"Captain, if the *Queen* will explode, it is not safe to remain aboard her lifeboats. They do not possess adequate propulsion to escape an explosion envelope of that magnitude. You must come board."

"I can't, *Recovery.* Keep your distance."

"But Captain, you will die."

"I know."

"I don't want you to die." The *Recovery's* voice sounded confused, like a child told her parent is going away and does not understand what that means.

"It's the only way, *Recovery.*"

"It is my duty to preserve your life, Ma'am."

"I know. I'm sorry." My face was wet. I was crying saying goodbye to my damned emotionless AI. "Give me the *Merryweather's* captain."

I pumped my legs faster to keep up with Walkabout. I was dizzy as hell—I checked my wrist, still bandaged, not seeping as far as I could tell. Good.

"Hello, Kira. Your AI tells me you're staying aboard that hulk and are threatening to blow it up. Listen, she's yours. You found her fair and square. I won't steal her." His voice was deep and unfamiliar.

"No time for that now, Captain. You need to get out of here."

"I'd leave you to it, Captain, but your ship is in pretty bad shape and it looks like that hulk isn't going anywhere. Let me give you a ride, or at least help you patch up your wave drive."

Hezu Christos I wanted to take him up on his offer. If only I could—

I ran faster. If we beat the Hand to the lifeboats . . . .

"Hold that thought, Captain. You see a lifeboat coming, you don't let it dock without my okay, you hear me?"

"Is there a reason I shouldn't?"

"You don't know the half of it." If I told the truth, he'd never believe me. I thought fast. "There's a space-mad killer over here who has rigged the *Queen* to explode. He's on his way to the last lifeboat. Do not let it dock with you until you know we beat him, hear me?"

"Loud and clear. Good luck, Captain."

"Be careful, Kira," *Recovery* said. "Your life signs are alarming."

I shut up and concentrated on keeping up with Walkabout—if I could stay focused and determined like her, we just might live through this. I checked the map on my viewpad. One more corner and we were there. We were a lot closer to the lifeboats than the bridge was. There was a chance.

"Wait." Walkabout stopped and motioned for the knife. I gave it to her. She knew how to use it better than I did. She gripped the thing, her mouth a fine line.

"I'm right behind you," I said, and I followed her into the airlock. No sign of the Hand. "Where is he?"

She showed me the viewpad.

Terraformer Mechanic Tobias Lovara: disembarked

"What the hell does that mean?"

Walkabout pointed outside. He was in space. Either already aboard the lifeboat, or crawling across the outer hull to save time. I checked my slit wrist and the tie on it and turned up my suit's blow all the way. I wouldn't have a seal, and what was left of my hand was going to be even more fekked, but I didn't have a choice. I rammed the glove on as best as I could, for whatever protection it could provide. I clung to the grab bar with my good hand and nodded.

Walkabout blew the lock. Again, I was buffeted by the air sucking in to vacuum. She looked left, then right, then reached for the cable. I looked too—no sign of the Hand. The lifeboat still bobbed at the end of the tether. She sheathed the knife and crawled down toward it. I was right behind her, jerking myself forward with one hand, looking all around in the black of space, over the *Queen's* hull, my breath echoing loud inside my helmet. It is fek-all hard to see out of an EVA, and I didn't see him anywhere.

We climbed into the lock and sealed it behind us. Walkabout gripped her knife.

"Ready?"

She nodded. I opened the inner lock.

The cockpit of the lifeboat was empty, except for the dangling cables where the AI used to be.

"Hezu Christos and all the multitudes. We beat him. Maybe he went to the wrong side, where the other lifeboats are." I slumped against the wall while Walkabout checked around, just to be sure. There wasn't any place for him to hide. She pushed some rations out of the chair and looked out the viewer, studying what she could see of the hull.

"I don't see him," she said and looked back at me. Her eyes scanned the bulkheads above and below, like she was trying to see through them.

No. He was not outside clinging to the lifeboat because I wasn't going to let him be. I refused to let him be. "Let's get the fek out of here. *Recovery*, can you hear me?"

"Yes, Captain."

"We beat him to the lifeboat. Here we come."

"Wait," Walkabout said, but I wasn't listening to her. I wanted to live. I launched us. I felt the strain of the cables, then we pulled free.

"What if he's on the hull? We can't take him with us. We can't."

The panic in her voice made me look out the airlock's tiny window again. No sign of him, but I couldn't see much of the outside and the lifeboat's limited sensors weren't designed to detect much more than the broad side of a planet. "He's not there," I said, trying to figure out how to make sure. "He's not with us."

"What if he is?" She pointed the knife at the window, her eyes hollow with everything she'd lived through.

I wanted to tell her she was paranoid, that she was wrong. I wanted to shout that we had escaped and left him behind. That we were going to live. Instead I only strapped myself in and watched the *Queen's* massive bulk dwindle behind us, until I could see the entire beehive again. There was nothing moving across her surface—no sign of the Hand.

"*Kira*," Walkabout said, "we have to get out and check the hull."

I shook my head. "We're moving too fast. It's not safe." Even if we did go out and look, he would take us—dominate our minds—if he was there, which he was not, because I wouldn't let him be. I felt the stress and Gs pressing me down into the seat.

I looked out the cockpit, over Walkabout's head. The *Recovery* was there, scorched. Next to her was, I presumed, the *Merryweather*. It was a sleek ship, like *Recovery*, built for finding, not for hauling booty.

"Captain, I am receiving a strange transmission," *Recovery* said.

"Strange how?"

"The sender says she is the *Queen*."

"Let it through."

"It is nearly time," a voice I thought I'd never hear again spoke, a clipped principal's tone. "Where is the Hand?"

"He went outside," I said. "We left him there somewhere on your hull. You're about to surprise the fek out of him, *Queen*. Walkabout and I are on the lifeboat. There's another ship out here. We're going to get away. She's going to live." I said it like a prayer. As if, by passionately believing it, I could make it true. The pressure built, a headache with it, like I was being flattened inside my own body.

"Praise Hezu. I'm glad. Please tell her I am glad to have known her. Please tell her goodbye again."

I told Walkabout, but she just nodded and didn't bother to wipe the wetness off her face.

"*Merryweather*, prepare to receive two new passengers. Then we need to get the fek out of here before this hulk blows."

"I read you, Captain," the deep voice said.

"*Queen*, what's your time table?"

"Six minutes."

"*Recovery*, does the *Merryweather* have room for you? Can

you transfer to one of her drives? We won't have time to fix you before the *Queen* blows. We'll have to all get out together."

"Yes, Captain. She has made an accommodation for me."

"Can you still talk to me using her communications?"

"I am now, Ma'am."

We were going to make it. The strain lifted, and I could think clearly again.

I hesitated.

If he really were on our lifeboat, escaping wouldn't do us any good. Finally, I let Walkabout's common sense penetrate my own panic. As much as I wanted to believe we were in the clear, I had to find out for sure.

"*Recovery*, have the *Merryweather* scan our hull." I said. "I need to know if there is anything on it. A body, maybe."

"Captain, your acceleration would make space walk una-vis—"

"I need to know, *Recovery*. Is there anyone clinging to the hull?"

"The *Merryweather* and I estimate there is insufficient time for a thorough scan. If you do not slow your acceleration and dock with us very soon, we will not be able to achieve minimum safe distance. Both vessels will be destroyed if we linger," Recovery said.

"We have to, *Recovery*, or none of this will matter." I felt the grim truth of my own words hanging in the air. "If there is a body clinging to the ship," I said, "I will have to abort our approach. I need you to get out of here with the *Merryweather* and leave us behind."

"Why?" *Recovery* asked.

Walkabout stared at me, unable to hear what *Recovery* was saying through my earpiece.

"What's happening?" Walkabout asked.

I ignored her, and knew *Recovery* wouldn't believe what Walkabout and I had been through—even if we had time to try and explain. "Biological contaminant. I can't dock with the *Merryweather* if it's with us. Eyeball us if you don't have time for anything else."

"Yes, Captain. Commencing visual scan."

I turned the boat slowly over as I guided us toward the *Merryweather's* lock. She was a small ship, like *Recovery*, but she'd be able to accommodate three just fine. We were going to live, unless I broke off in the next few seconds and pulled away. If *Recovery* saw something I'd tell them to leave us to the explosion. "*Recovery*? What do you see? I need to know right now."

"There are no biological contaminants detected, Captain," *Recovery* said. "Proceed with docking maneuvers. We must leave in two minutes."

I let out the breath I was holding.

"Kira?" Walkabout asked.

"We're clean." I smiled at her and engaged the auto-docking program. The boat connected and the seal pressurized. I felt us begin to accelerate as the *Merryweather* fired her own engines and started taking us out of there.

"Hello, Captain. Is it safe?" *Merryweather's* captain asked.

"Yes. Just me and one innocent survivor. A kid. Just warning you—we stink like hell."

He laughed. He had a nice voice.

"Is this really happening?" Walkabout's eyes were wide as we entered the air lock together.

"Yes." I smiled at her. "We're getting out of here." I activated the lock. It slid open. The captain of the *Merryweather* looked through the window at us and I heard the hiss of the decontamination jets as they washed over us. I waved with my good arm. The lock opened. *Merryweather's* captain had his gun out, but he smiled nervously and stepped back. Balding, with a bit of a belly, but he had a nice face. He was in a plaid robe and a pair of slippers. Pretty much what I usually wore.

"Thanks, Captain," I said. "Shall we?" I turned and realized Walkabout had stepped back into the lifeboat.

"Something's wrong." Walkabout stood still, holding onto a handful of useless wires in the lifeboat's cockpit.

Something swollen and frozen *thunked* against the cockpit window behind Walkabout.

It was a human hand.

"*Recovery!*" I shouted.

"I am programmed to preserve human life, Captain, even against orders. Your fear of corpses is illogical. You must—" *Recovery* interrupted herself. "—insufficient resources."

"*Recovery?*"

"Insufficient resources."

Then Walkabout swayed in place. "Something's pressing on me . . . ." Her words trailed off and her mouth gaped open. The demon was trying for her. Even through the compreglass, he was trying for her.

"No! No, no, no." I lunged back inside the lifeboat but tripped and landed on my knees. I grabbed her and hugged her. "Fight him, Walkabout. You fight."

She trembled in my arms, shaking like a bad engine. Her mouth moved, wordless.

"Kira? What's going on?" *Merryweather's* captain shouted above the sound of the decontamination jets. I ignored him.

"You fight." I watched her eyes. She was losing. The Hand was taking over. I felt her move her arms and I looked down.

She held up a small black box. I looked into her eyes and saw her determination. She was going to do it.

"Fek no. Oh fek." I dragged her into the *Merryweather* through the sanitizing mist, bumping into her captain, who backed out of our way. "Close the lock!" I kept going, past him, past the rim of the outer lock, as deep into the *Merryweather* as I could go, and grabbed onto a rail. If I could get Walkabout away from him she would beat him. I knew she would. I wouldn't let her fail.

"Walkabout."

She didn't answer.

"Elizabet, please!"

Her mouth moved silently. I leaned close to make out her words.

"Everyone's dead," she whispered with her last breath. And I watched the Hand beat her, and the light go out of her eyes.

The box slipped from her lifeless fingers, and they spasmed a second too late to catch it. It bounced once on the deck, then detonated the explosives rigged all over the lifeboat's exterior.

Flames blew passed me and I slammed into the deck. My EVA squealed alarms and my useless hand lost hold of Walkabout. Then, just as suddenly as I was blown forward, I was sucked backward. As I scrambled to grab something, anything, my limbs skidded across the deck. Then I caught hold of the edge of a bolted-down cabinet. The docking compartment of the *Merryweather* emptied of air, sucking out the hole blown in the lock. Alarms sounded and the warning lights flashed. The force of it bowed my head toward my feet. I had a clear view of a small body in a white juvenile suit tumbling away into space, moving its arms and legs, the Hand trying one last time to save itself inside Walkabout. A plaid body tumbled not too far away from it—I had never even learned his name. There were more body parts—legs, an arm, wearing the burnt remains of a colonizer uniform. The shattered remains of the lifeboat shot backward, tumbling, falling toward the *Queen*. The vector of the explosion had blown the *Merryweather* away from the colonizer. She shrank, and I saw *Recovery's* shell spinning off in another direction.

Then the *Queen* exploded.

Walkabout's white form disappeared against the brightness of the explosion. My faceplate darkened to automatically protect me from the light, but it seared into my eyes, the new sun dawning. The *Merryweather's* fire control protection kicked in, and the bulkhead doors came crashing shut, sealing me off from the ruined docking compartment and the expanding *Queen*. The *Merryweather's* engines fired—she was trying to save me.

Then the shockwave hit her, and I banged all around inside as the ship rode the wave, tumbling over and over. It was an endless nightmare of rolling. A minute became more, and I lost track in the senseless spinning. My brains scrambled inside my head. I think I passed out.

Finally, the *Merryweather* stilled and righted herself with maneuvering thrusters. There was no sound. I lay blinking for a long time. There wasn't a part of my body that didn't hurt.

The first question on my mind, right after figuring out if I were really alive, was if I were really alone. Was there a way for the Hand to reach me through the black void? There was only one thing I could think of to protect myself from him. It had worked before.

"*Recovery.*"

"Yes, Captain."

"Report."

"The *Queen* has been destroyed. The *Merryweather* has rudimentary propulsion. She is sorrowing for her captain; she was with him a long time."

"Tell her I'm sorry."

"Captain, protocol states we should—"

"Shut up." I wanted to rage at her. I wanted to scream that it was her fault Walkabout was dead, and that she'd nearly killed us all with her damned superior AI brains. But it wouldn't do any good. She wouldn't understand, and it wasn't really true anyway. Instead I lay there and cried.

"I'm so sorry, Captain." *Recovery* said after endless minutes of no sound but my own echoing sobs. The sentiment almost sounded real.

"I need you to play something for me, and you need to keep playing it, you hear me? Also, you and *Merryweather* need to use every sensor you have to comb the outside of this ship. I don't care if it's a corpse or a hunk of metal—anything that doesn't belong to you, you report."

They did. There were no bodies. Only mine. *Recovery* obliged me and played what I asked. I also instructed them to destroy the ship if they detected any hacking. Some other searcher would come and find us. I hoped whoever that was found us before they found the Hand, wherever it was now, so I could give warning. The modeling program the AIs created predicted a ninety-nine point six percent chance that that the body of Walkabout, the *Merryweather's* Captain, and the corpse clinging to the lifeboat had been pulled into the gravity well of the small star created after the Queen exploded. In theory, we were safe. But I'd been safe before. Or thought I was. I hadn't listened to Walkabout, and she'd been right. She'd been right the whole time, about everything.

As I was in the medical bay administering the anesthetic to myself, I told my story to the AIs and had them record it for posterity. They promised to transmit it and a complete record of the whole incident toward the nearest relay station.

"Everyone's dead—" a high, child's voice continued to cycle from *Merryweather's* speakers like a protective talisman. I couldn't trust the small ship AIs to understand the meaning of sacrifice for the greater good, so I hoped the voice was right and everyone and everything that had been aboard the *Queen* really was dead. That thought brought me comfort as I thrust both wrists under the laser saw and amputated my hands. Walkabout's voice echoed over the sound of searing flesh, a small defiant human noise against the vast darkness outside.

THE CORNERS HAVE ARMS

JEREMY HEPLER

Sophie flicked her cigarette butt out the car window and checked her cell phone. It was 2AM. Fifteen minutes since her last text. Time for another.

WHERE R MY BABIES???

She didn't expect a reply.

Carlos hadn't answered his cell or replied to her texts in twenty-four hours. Motherfucker. She never should've allowed him to take the twins to the valley. Never. No matter how excited they were to visit that farm house again. No matter how much they begged and gave her the sad eyes. No matter how many times Carlos assured her everything would be fine, that they'd call every day. She should've never given in. She knew better.

In the months before the divorce, when the fights had become verbally vicious and occasionally physical, Carlos had threatened to sneak the twins across the border and hide them from her. *Raise them the right way. Far away from her worthless ass.* But Judge Wharton either didn't believe her or didn't care when she'd told him about the threats. He'd ordered that Carlos get the twins every other weekend during the school year, and two weeks of the summer.

His two weeks were up at noon yesterday. And he hadn't brought the girls home as promised.

Sophie blotted her swollen eyes with the bottom of her T-shirt, lit another cigarette, and took a lengthy puff. Remembering. Regretting.

The last time she'd talked to one of the girls was Thursday evening, the night before they were supposed to come home.

Nine-year-old Cecilia had acted odd on the phone that night. She had been uncharacteristically bland and short with her greeting, and when Sophie asked what she and Monica were up to, how their day was going, she'd stayed quiet for a long moment, whispered something to someone else, and then said, "I can't talk right now, Mom." And hung up.

Sophie called right back, and it took Carlos nearly twenty rings to answer. Of course, he blamed her for Cecilia's behavior. She let the girls stay up as late as they wanted, wear what they wanted, eat in front of the TV, talk back. Worse, she let them watch those violent horror movies, and read zombie comics and Harry Potter books. If they were acting rude or strange, it was entirely her fault.

Sophie squeezed the steering wheel hard, gritted her teeth, the cords in her neck tightening. Fucking Carlos. To him, *everything* was her fault. The girls' troubles focusing at school. Their lack of manners and friends. The divorce. His high blood pressure, sleep problems, impotency. Everything.

She released a clutched breath and glanced at the picture of Cecilia and Monica on her cell phone. They were dressed as witches, their laughing faces pressed together. She took a drag and shook her head, disgusted at herself for not demanding Carlos put Cecilia back on the phone that night.

Cecilia had never acted like that before. She usually loved gabbing with Mom, enthusiastically explaining her day's events as though they affected the entire world. And she'd never hung up without saying, "Loves, hugs, and kisses." Neither of the girls had.

"She was reaching out to me," Sophie blurted out. "And what did *I* do?" She tapped her chest hard enough to make a thud, then glanced at herself in the rearview mirror. Her eyes brimming with tears. "What did *I* do? Her *Mom*. I didn't do shit. Not a damn thing."

She pushed down harder on the gas pedal, brought the speed of the Toyota Corolla, she'd been awarded in the divorce settlement, up to ninety. "I'm coming, baby," she said with motherly conviction. "And I'll fucking kill him if he's done anything to you. I swear to God I will."

* * *

Normally the drive from Flat Rock to the valley took nine hours, but Sophie made it in less than eight. She turned on FM 32 as the sun was rising in a puddle of gold and pink.

When the giant house and long rows of lemon and avocado trees bracketing it came into view, she saw Carlos' cherry red Yukon parked in the long curved driveway, and the tension that had been pressing down on her chest since yesterday afternoon lessened its burden. But only slightly. Because she didn't see Eloy's car anywhere.

Eloy, Carlos's twin brother, was supposed to stay at the house the entire two weeks the girls were there. He'd been there two days ago. Playing Checkers with Monica according to Carlos.

What if they took Eloy's car? What if they took it across…

Eloy had a house in Matamoras, a second somewhere near Mexico City, and a third somewhere on the west coast. Or at least he claimed to. And per Carlos's threats before the divorce, Eloy had connections with the corrupt Mexican police and government. He had Mexican citizenship. And his car, a Yukon similar to Carlos', had Mexican plates. He had everything they needed to blend in, become instantly Mexican, disappear forever.

The smidgen of tension that had slipped off Sophie's chest when she'd first seen Carlos' Yukon not only returned, but also returned with vigor. She parked behind the Yukon, killed the engine, fished the 9MM out of the glovebox, and then glanced at herself in the rearview mirror.

She looked haggard, way older than thirty-one. Her skin

was blotchy, eyes wired with nicotine yet puffy from crying. Her hair was wild and frizzy. Carlos would say she looked disgraceful. *Trashy. Nasty.* Like the strung-out transient hooker he'd helped get off the streets ten years earlier. That she should be ashamed to step out of the house like this. But fuck Carlos. She wasn't here for him.

She wedged the 9MM in the back waistband of her jeans and marched toward the front door, scanning the windows on the first floor for signs of movement. When she stepped onto the porch, her stomach seemed to flip upside down. She hated this house. Had vowed never to step foot inside it again after what had happened last time she was here. For her girls, though, she'd do it. For them, she'd do anything. They were all she had in the world.

Sophie pounded on the front door five hard times. "Carlos!" she yelled, then pounded five more. "Cecilia! Monica!"

She stepped back and surveyed the second floor windows. Maybe they were upstairs. She'd spent enough time in the house to know you couldn't hear much of anything going on downstairs if you were up there. She pounded on the door again, then tried the knob and found it unlocked.

The stench of ammonia—*fucking cat piss*—assaulted her nose when she stepped into the foyer, and her nasal cavities immediately collapsed.

Carlos's mom, Aurora, had inherited the house in the mid-70s, lived there until her death, and in her will passed it to her twin sons, who now used it as a vacation house. She had insisted on keeping seven cats in the house at all times—the perfect number to ward off *espiritus malignos* and *brujas maliciosas*. She'd named the cats after saints, and Carlos and Eloy had insisted on keeping them after her death. Litter boxes abound.

Sophie hated the cats. She hated their dander, their stink, the way they watched her with callous, hunting eyes, seemingly eager to pounce and slash. And she absolutely couldn't stand the noises the females made at night while in heat. Screaming and howling as though their warm insides were being ripped out. The nights she'd stayed there, she'd laid in bed and dug her fingernails into her thighs, praying for them to stop.

"Cecilia? Monica?" Sophie called out as she closed the front door.

A thick, unsettling silence swallowed her words.

She made her way into the sitting room and turned on the floor lamp. The room looked exactly as it had the last time she was here. Flower-patterned couches faced one another in the center of the room, two matching chairs between them, all four covered in cat hair. One of Aurora's Santeria talismans hung on the far wall in the center of a slew of family photos, collecting dust.

Sophie left the room and walked past the staircase and entered the master bedroom, which was the lone bedroom on the floor. It was still crammed with the boxes Sophie and the girls had packed two summers ago, stacked five-feet high in places, all labeled with one word: AURORA.

She moved on to the living room. When she turned on a lamp sitting on an end table and saw her daughter's Hello Kitty jackets draped over the tan sectional, the pink sleeves glistening in the halogen, she picked them up and pressed them to her nose, sniffing, hoping to catch a whiff of the girls' strawberry shampoo, or Princess Perfume, but her nose was too clogged. Fucking cats.

Holding the jackets to her chest, she headed to the eat-in-kitchen and adjoining dining room. Two glasses with faint milk rings were on the island in the center of the kitchen. She touched one. It felt warm, unused for many hours. All the other dishes and cookware were clean and neatly stacked in the doorless cupboards. All the chairs pushed under the tables, place mats perfectly aligned, Carlos-Style. Aurora's pouch of dried bay leaves—*maleta de curacion*— dangled from a hook above the sink, no longer fragrant.

Sophie pushed the pouch aside and looked out the kitchen window to check the swing set behind the house. Nothing. No beautiful twins laughing and playing. Just ghosts swinging in the wind.

She moved on. Checked the main bathroom. The laundry room.

With each empty room and unanswered call, the silence grew heavier, Sophie's chest tighter. Making it harder to breathe. Hard not to assume and embrace the heart-wrenching worst.

He did it. He took them to fucking Mexico.

She hurried back to the staircase and headed upstairs, calling out the girls' names again and again.

She was greeted on the carpeted landing by two cats— Odilo and Stephen, called O and Steve, if she remembered correctly. Blocking her way, Steve stared at her like a hungry predator. She swung the girls' jackets at him and told him to get, which he did, scurrying down the hall with O close behind.

The bedroom the girls used, the largest of three upstairs, was on the far end of the hall. Sophie hurried to the door, opened it, and turned on the light. The king-sized bed the girls shared was made. The same hideous grapevine bedspread covering it. A talisman with an azabache pebble in the center hung above the headboard. The blinds over the two windows were closed.

As Sophie's eyes moved toward the adjoining bathroom, a slight simper found her lips. The girls' Teen Titan Raven backpacks were leaning against the wall next to the door. And they looked full. She rushed over to them, unzipped one, dug inside. She found Monica's Leap Pad, Snoopy doll, costume jewelry, and her notebook of drawings. Monica never went anywhere without her drawings.

But then where…

Suddenly, a horrific possibility seized Sophie's heart like a clamp, squeezed down tight like a muscle. The blackness of it filling her lungs, the tentacles wringing her bowels.

Maybe they hadn't gone anywhere. Maybe Carlos had…

She squeezed her eyes tight and shook her head as though she could jar the horrible thought from her mind. But she couldn't. It kept growing, rooting deeper, demanding acknowledgement. She rushed into the bathroom. Two toothbrushes in the holder. Two purple robes hanging on a hook behind the door. A tube of Sparkle toothpaste and a hair brush on the counter. She cupped her mouth.

What if he killed them?

There it was. Out in the open. An option worse than the worst. One she'd been hiding from herself all day. But she'd watched enough ID Channel to know it happened. A spouse putting a bullet in everyone's head for revenge. Out of spite. But Carlos wasn't the type. He loved the girls. He wouldn't—couldn't—do that to them. Could he?

Oh, God.

Sophie ran out of the room and down the hall, screaming her babies' names as loud as her dry throat would allow. She pushed open each bedroom door, flicked on every light. Found every room empty and silent.

When she reached the door closest to the staircase, the office door, she took in a deep breath before she flung it open. That room, too, was empty. Of humans anyway. A cat—Paul, she knew because of his striped tail—was standing on a desk next to Carlos's laptop.

Carlos never went anywhere without his laptop.

Sophie screeched and knocked the laptop off the desk. It crashed onto the floor, the screen snapping off the base. Paul leapt to the floor and bolted up the open doorway leading to the attic.

The attic.

The girls' castle.

Sophie followed Paul up the stairs and called the girls' names.

A stream of light shooting through the round window lit half the attic with yellow sunlight. The other half was dark.

She could hear cats moving around. One skittered across the beam of light and jumped through a window on Cecilia and Monica's playhouse. Carlos and Eloy had built the castle-themed playhouse when the girls were five. It was painted like stones, complete with a small plywood drawbridge that could be lowered by a flimsy crank. Carlos had even put a sink inside with running water. Battery-run torch lights hung on the walls inside, giving the place an orange glow.

Sophie was running her hand along the wall, searching for the light switch, when Carlos called out.

"Don't turn it on."

Sophie's heart fluttered and her hand froze.

Seconds later, a lantern lit on the dark side of the attic. Carlos was sitting in a wooden chair holding the lantern, five feet from the castle. His hair was disheveled, not slicked back and gelled as usual. And his slacks and Guayabera were wrinkled, not starched, crisp as frost on grass, as he usually insisted.

"Where are the girls?" Sophie asked, marching toward him.

He locked his tired eyes on hers, but didn't answer.

She stopped in front of him, pulled out the 9MM, pointed it at his face.

"I'm so glad you came," he said, his voice caged with stress. "I'm losing my mind here."

"Where are they?" Sophie asked. "What did you do?"

"I didn't do anything. And get that fucking slut gun out of my face." Carlos swatted at the gun, but Sophie moved back out of his reach.

She had acquired the 9MM from a guy named Big Fly when she was fourteen and in foster care. Traded ten blow jobs for the gun and a handful of bullets. Carlos had always called it her slut gun. She called it the best insurance policy on the market. The big brother she never had. A guarantee she would walk out of any hotel room or car in one piece. Wouldn't get robbed or cheated. And would rest a little better when sleep found her.

"Where are my babies, Carlos?" Her hands growing sweaty, voice desperate. "Where's Eloy?"

"*Eloy?* He left yesterday morning. He had a meeting in Mexico. Why?"

"Are they with him?"

"No."

"Then where are they?" A beat. "Did you hurt them? I swear to God if you—"

"I didn't hurt them," Carlos cut in, standing up and puffing out his chest in protest. "I would never hurt them. You should know that."

"All I *know* is that you were supposed to bring them home yesterday and you didn't. And that you haven't responded to my texts or calls in twenty-four fucking hours."

Carlos inhaled and exhaled loudly, combed his fingers through his hair. "I didn't answer your calls because I didn't know what to say without sounding bat-shit crazy, okay? I knew you wouldn't believe me. You have to hear it for yourself." He sat back down, shook his head, seemingly discouraged, beaten.

"Hear what?"

Carlos glanced into the darkness beyond the playhouse, back at Sophie.

Sophie's chest began to burn, as though a fire had been lit inside her heart. "What?"

No reply.

"*What!?*" The flames hotter, doused with gasoline. She aimed the gun at the ceiling and fired.

Carlos dropped the lantern and jumped up, knocking the chair down as he back-peddled. "What the hell are you doing? You could've...We don't know if...Don't do that!" He rushed at Sophie, grabbed her arm with one hand, the barrel of the gun with the other.

"Where are they?" Sophie yelled as they struggled for control of the gun. "Where are my babies?"

"I don't know," Carlos said. "But if you calm the fuck down and listen, you'll hear them. They keep calling for *you* anyway."

Sophie gave pause long enough for Carlos to jerk the gun free. Then he threw his forearm into her chest, knocking her to the floor.

Teetering on the edge of Meltdown Cliff, she slammed her palms down onto the floor over and over like a tantrum toddler. "What do you mean calling for me? What are you talking about? What is going on? Where are they, Carlos? Where are they?" Her heavy breathing gave way to hot tears, and she pulled her knees to her chest.

Carlos picked up the lantern, crouched in front of her, and let her sob for a moment before speaking. "You have to listen to me, okay? I know this will sound insane," he said. "I still don't fully believe it myself." He took in a shaky breath and pushed it out. "But I think they're trapped in the darkness somewhere...in the corner." He gestured with the gun toward the dark corner behind the castle.

"*What?*"

"I know...I know...I can't explain it. I can't...I don't know. I don't know what is..."

"You're full of shit. You *know* where they are."

"I swear to God, Soph, I don't." Tears formed in his eyes. "They were up here playing yesterday morning, and when it was time to go, I came up to get them and they weren't here. I freaked out and searched everywhere and when I couldn't find them, I came back up here and that's when I heard them." He pointed at the corner again. His hand and the gun trembling. "Over there."

Sophie scrutinized him with skeptical eyes. He was good at pretending, acting. Lying. He'd majored in theater at UT, dreamed of making it big on Broadway someday. But he'd given up on that dream by the age of twenty-two and had decided to become a high school Theater Arts teacher instead. A decision he refused to discuss or expand on when Sophie brought it up. She had never seen him perform on stage, but Eloy and many others had bragged of his talent.

"You better not be lying to me, Carlos."

"I swear on my mom I'm not lying. Or playing or teasing or acting. I'm either losing my mind, or something fucked-up is going on here." He licked his lips, shook his head. "I *heard* them, Soph. In that corner. I *heard* them calling for you. But...they're not there. I don't know if...I just don't know, okay? I don't have any answers. You need to go over there and listen. Please."

Sophie glanced at the 9MM, and he followed her eyes. "If I wanted to shoot you, I would've already," he said. She stared at him, and eventually, he tossed the gun to the opposite side of the attic, sending cats scurrying in the darkness. "There. Happy?"

Sophie stood. "Give me the lantern."

"If you take a light over there they won't talk. I've tried."

A long silence spooled out, then Sophie took a step toward the corner. Another step. Another. Looked back at Carlos. He hadn't moved, was watching her. As they held eye contact:

"Mommy?"

"Mom?"

From the corner.

Sophie's heart leapt up into her throat.

"Did you hear that?" Carlos asked, standing and pointing.

Sophie couldn't find her voice to answer. She could barely breathe.

Though the words landed faintly in her ears, barley a whisper, Sophie could tell the twins apart. Only a mother could. The first voice was Monica. Cecilia, the second.

"Mom? Are you there?"

"Mom?...Help us."

Help—a word Sophie both loved (they *need* me, they *need* their Mom) and hated (dear God, they *need* me).

"I'm coming, baby," she said, making her way deeper into the darkness, closer and closer to the voices coming from the corner.

Help.

She put her hands out in front of her, found the wall, the sharp angle of the corner. It sounded like the girls' voices were coming from somewhere far beyond the wall. Like Carol Anne in that scary show Sophie and the girls had watched on Netflix. In the house, yet somehow not.

"How do I get there?" Sophie yelled, slapping at the wall as though it were purposefully blocking her from her girls. She had to be dreaming. She ran her hands along the wall, probing for a secret doorknob or magical button. Anything. She glanced back at Carlos. He was staring her way. "Where are they?" she yelled.

He didn't answer. When she turned back toward the corner, something cold suddenly seized her by the neck. A hand. A cold strong hand attached to a cold strong arm extending from the wall.

She frantically grabbed at the hand, trying to wrench it loose. Then a second arm looped around her waist and jerked her against the wall. The hand grabbed at her love handles, pinched down like a pair of thick flat pliers. Twisted the flesh a bit. She cried out in pain, in fear, in absolute shock and disbelief. She called out for Carlos as the hand around her neck squeezed tighter, pulled her head against the wall harder.

Carlos was there in a second. She felt his warm hands on her shoulders. But he didn't try to pull her away from the corner, away from the cold arms and hands. Instead, he shoved her into the corner, pinned her to the sheetrock like a poster. "Take her! Take her now!" he yelled, smashing her face into the wall so hard her bottom lip split open, leaking the taste of copper into her mouth.

The corner's hands held tight, pulled, pinched, choked. Carlos pushed and jammed, using his knees as well as his hands now. As Sophie struggled, the wall began to feel cold and wet, soft, giving way in places. A porous portal opening between two worlds. Her daughter's calls grew closer, louder, clearer.

Sophie's left leg and arm slipped into the unnatural softness first, sending gooseflesh skittering up her skin. The darkness seemed to have ten hands on her now, tugging, pulling. Wanting.

Carlos reared back and shove the back of her head, forcing the rest of her body to dip into the softness.

Somewhere between the Hernandez attic and her daughter's desperate calls, she stumbled forward, arms outstretched, pushed by the hands now, blinded by black, hollering back to her girls.

When she emerged from the disorienting darkness, she fell to her knees. She was still in the attic, though it wasn't the *real* attic. The entire place, every object in sight, the girl's castle playhouse, the walls, the door leading downstairs to Carlos's office, all seemed to be covered in a thin sepia film. Like the photo they'd taken in western clothes at Six Flags two years ago.

As she rubbed her eyes, trying to get them to focus, a small hand touched her arm.

"Mom?"

Her eyes snapped open. It was Cecilia. Sepia-toned Cecilia. But Cecilia.

Sophie grabbed her daughter, pulled her to her chest, closed her eyes and squeezed hard. As though she could squish Cecilia into her, mesh together as one. Then she heard, "Mommy," and felt Monica press up against her side. Sophie looped one arm around Monica. Tears falling down her cheeks. A relieved sensation oozing through her body. She didn't care where they were. They were together. She'd found her babies.

Cecilia and Monica pulled away, and Sophie stooped to see them at eye level. She combed Monica's shoulder-length hair with one hand, stroked Cecilia's cheek with the other.

"Are you girls all right?" Sophie asked, her eyes sliding from Monica to Cecilia.

They both nodded. Flat expressions, baffled eyes. She gave them each another quick, solid hug, and then turned around and touched the dark corner she'd passed through. It was firm. No softness. No cold. No needy hands. She glanced at the girls who were standing still as statues in their summer dresses, watching her. "Is the whole house like this? This color, I mean."

Again, they nodded.

"What about outside?"

"We can't go outside," Cecilia said. "The doors don't work. But—" She broke off when Monica nudged her.

"But what?" Sophie asked.

The girls stared at her, fighting back words seemingly eager to leap off their tongues.

"Girls?"

No answer.

"*Girls?*"

As the girls spoke to one another with their eyes the way only twins can, Sophie heard soft footfalls coming up the stairs that lead to Carlos's office. She turned and saw Aurora stride into the attic. She was wearing a floor-length skirt and short-sleeve button-up. Her long grey hair in a tight bun, arms stiff at her sides—the same way she'd looked and walked whether outside inspecting lemon trees or cooking in the kitchen. Her favorite cat Thomas (Tom-Tom) strutted beside her on three feet. Still missing the paw on his front right leg—the same shriveled paw that Aurora wore on a string around her neck, hidden under her clothing.

Sophie's legs turned to flimsy matchsticks at the sight.

"Come here girls," Aurora said. "Give Abuela a hug."

The girls' eyes flitted from the ground to their mom a few times before they hurried over to Aurora and wrapped their arms around her.

Sophie braced herself against the wall with her hand. Sepia Aurora—Dead Aurora— eyed her with the dreadful pleasure.

"Get away from them," Sophie said, so faint she barely heard herself. "Get away from them." Louder this time.

"What, dear?" Aurora asked.

Sophie steadied herself, pushed away from the wall, fisted

her hands and locked her knees. "Get away from them!"

A broad grin spread across Aurora's face. The Bitch Grin. The one she'd given Sophie anytime Carlos's back was turned. Anytime the girls had taken her side over Sophie's. The Bitch Grin. The one she'd flashed even in her waning days when the cancer was devouring her insides, when Sophie was forced by Carlos to live at the house and tend to her every need. The one she flashed after each cussing she gave Sophie, each slap, each thrown plate of food.

Sophie stormed toward Aurora and jerked the girls back, gripping their arms much harder than intended. "Don't touch my girls!"

Monica and Cecilia ran toward the dark corner that Sophie had come through. Their eyes full of hurt—hurt only a mom's disapproval can conjure. Cecilia rubbed her arm.

"I'm sorry," Sophie said. "I didn't mean to grab you so hard. But she— "

"It'll be okay, girls," Aurora butted in.

Sophie thrust an accusatory finger in Aurora's face. "Don't you ever tell my girls it'll be okay. I tell them when it's okay. You have no right."

Holding Sophie's gaze, Aurora slightly cocked her head and angled her brows in a gesture of pity—the kind of pity shown to a clueless simpleton. Then she looked over at the girls and smiled. A sincere smile this time. "You did a great job, girls. You can go now. Tell your dad I'm proud of him, and that he hasn't lost his touch."

Aurora raised her thin hand into the air and snapped, and

the darkness in the corner behind Cecilia and Monica began to fluctuate, bend, soften. Two hands materialized, growing out of the blackness. Cecilia took one, Monica the other. They laced their free hands together, gave their mom a curt glance, and then shuffled into the wall.

Sophie's vision wobbled, followed by her stomach. No. The girls. Her babies.

What the...did they...practice...no...

She stumbled to the corner, but it was too late. The wall was already hard. Solid. There. "Cecilia? Monica?" she hollered.

She turned her ear to the wall, listening.

"Abuela said we did great, Daddy," Monica said.

"So do we get our prize?" Cecilia added.

"Of course," Carlos said. "Let's go."

The girls whooped and clapped, and within seconds, their cheering faded away. Far away.

Gone.

Sophie collapsed onto the floor in an awkward twist, howling and wailing like a cat in heat. Like her warm insides were being ripped out.

"Oh, you'll like it here," Aurora said, rubbing her hands together with glee. She walked slowly over to Sophie, jerked her upright by the hair, and covered her mouth and nose with a cold hand that smelled like cat piss. "How does it feel, *whore*? Not being able to breathe."

Sophie struggled to cry out, to break free, but Aurora's strength was inhuman, unnatural.

"When you shoved that spoon full of apple sauce and

Oxycontin down my throat and pressed that pillow to my face the last time you were here," Aurora said. "You did me the biggest favor of my life. You bound me to this house. And," That Bitch Grin, "you created a link that will bond us forever." She closed her eyes, hissed something in Spanish, then opened them. "Had you not killed me, I would've slipped deep into the spirit world, and I never would've been able to save my granddaughters from you."

Sophie's lights were going out. Lack of oxygen. Overwhelming sense of dread and panic. An assault of heartbreak and betrayal. Her legs buckled, and Aurora let her fall to the ground.

"Get up," Aurora demanded a moment later, kicking at Sophie's ribs. "You're fine. It's not like you can *really* die here."

THE CASE OF YURI ZAYSTEV

S.L. EDWARDS

Days were measured in piling snow, lives in black-rotting cells and time in final breaths. The white-washed landscape was the endless world. To walk there, in that featureless and terrible place, was to take a step toward heaven or hell. To stay there was to consign fate to the primal elements that were both God and Devil. The tundra existed before man walked, before reptiles crawled on the ocean floor, and would be there when the sun blots out and the earth becomes silent.

The only refuge from the cold, unchanging place was even worse than the vast frozen desert. Death was written into the architecture of the outpost before the endless night-world, a prison where men were sent to rot and disappear in fog and ice. It was more secret than Kolyma, built in a place where no men had ever visited before. Here, spit froze before it fell to the ground, while blood turned solid in two months time. Deprived of food and sunlight, men became slower and slower until they ceased to move at all.

Then, comrade Yuri Zaystev would have his job to do.

Yuri would drive the bodies of overworked and starved corpses into the frozen wasteland. Breath coming out as steam and no matter how hard he tried, feet numbing from cold, he would dump the bodies from the bed of his truck to form a pile in the snow. There was no need to bury corpses or hide transgressions against human life. The tundra winds would claim the human refuse, wrap it back into its cold folds and hide the bodies far away from human eyes and memory. Wiping itself clean the tundra would revert back to the untouched state it had always been in. There would be no records. The men condemned to this eternal exile had been marked dead before they even marched through the overbearing graveyard gates of the prison.

He had never found bodies or tracks in the tundra.

It was sunless, the night sky hung over Yuri as he listened to the desperate hum of a coughing motor. Through his foggy cab window Yuri could see the countless stars and heavenly bodies watching him, shining more brightly and more beautifully than they did anywhere else in the world. The only joy in his work was being with the quiet sky. Gone was the nervousness of Moscow, the fear of being called a dissident or traitor by some hungry neighbor. Gone was the fear of his mother being taken away, of joining his father in some death-camp on some other island of the Gulag Archipelago. Out there, alone, he could breathe freely and easily despite the frigid air that choked out all other life.

Ice crunched under his tires as he went farther into the Arctic Circle. Being in a vehicle created the sensation of false warmth, something he could not even dredge up from a flask of Vodka. The alcohol hit his stomach like gasoline and made him moan in discomfort. There was a difference between *burning* and heat. Cold could *burn*. The Vodka had been a bad idea, but monotony was the eternal enemy of the Gulag-grave digger.

He stopped his truck.

This spot was as good as any other.

The moon was brilliant, but in the featureless landscape the light did little for Yuri. He huffed, leaving the cab of his truck and bracing for the beastly winter that lived only in the Arctic Circle. He laughed, cursed and left the cab. His boots met the snow and beneath his many layers of fur and fat, his skeleton felt a chill that no amount of tendon or blood could stop.

In the tundra, he was no longer the young foot soldier. He was not the hero of Stalingrad, the boy who read to his little sister on her deathbed, or the young man who stood quietly by and said nothing when they took away his father while his mother howled. He was not culpable for what he was under the latitudes of the true north, not out there. Under the moonlight and the watchful eyes of Heaven, Yuri Zaystev was only flesh and bone.

The truck was large, given the amount of passengers he was ferrying that night. Recently, the camp had opened its mouth even wider to gluttonous portions of useless flesh. Whereas before there had been a trickle of people, now there was a torrential flow of traitors and criminals. Starvation was spreading from man to man; prisoners were now walking skeletons that did not have the will or strength to strangle each other for food as they did in warmer parts of Siberia. Yuri guessed he probably had twenty "people" in the back of his truck.

As he went to open the bed, Yuri had a drunken, evil thought. Part of him envied these men, who would be given a burial unlike any other. They died in this place, so far away from man and so close to God. In the tundra it was far too cold for their bodies to decay. If they were not eaten by polar bears, the winds would be kind to them and strip them of their skin until their bones were as white and gleaming as snow. When they became cracked-bone dust, they would be indistinguishable from the endless world around them.

They would become part of something much bigger than themselves.

He swung open the canvas-covered cab.

The thoughts came slowly. Yuri looked dumbly at the empty bed of the truck, expecting to blink back the bodies that were supposed to be there. The alcohol felt like it had been harshly sucked from his blood into his intestines, leaving him nauseous. Still in front of the gigantic, empty coffin-truck, he swallowed, completely sobered.

There weren't any bumps, no way for the bodies to be jostled out. He breathed heavily, remembering that he and Fyodor had loaded the corpses into the truck meticulously, carefully with the sacred silence of broken men. He laughed stupidly, remembering that they had first taken off the clothes of each corpse so that the worn garments could be recycled and given to a lucky few in the horde of new misfortunate prisoners. They had found food, knives, silverware in the pockets of rags and tatters.

He touched his forehead, covered though it was, and looked around him. There was nothing, not in the whole world.

He ran back to his cab, stumbling and struggling for the radio between gulping, wet breaths. Finding it, he removed his glove into the biting-knife cold and pushed the black button to speak.

"This is Private First-Class Yuri Zaystev. I am without cargo. Has something happened?"

He kept the radio on, ready for the voice of the Gulag to hiss back. The little red eye blinked, and blinked, and blinked. Static sparked, crackled and flared. A noise came through, something like a trumpet filled with water gurgled out of the speaker. Yuri remembered thundering mortars and flaring grenades and the noise rose to a shattering crescendo. It seemed as if there was one incoherent, inhuman voice that spoke along with the gibberish of the radio static. He could hear it crying as he pressed his hands to his covered ears to protect himself from the unwelcome, unwholesome sound. The speaker cracked, and once again silence reigned supreme.

He looked outside nervously. The black outside was absolute, unintelligible and without answer. Everything was still; even the stars had stopped shining and maintained a constant, somehow feebler light. There was no sound of weather, faint or otherwise. For a ponderous moment Yuri gained a new understanding of the word "quiet." It was more dreadful than screaming, moaning or pleas for help. It was far more unsettling and haunting to be perfectly and pristinely clean of noise, than to hear a man speak through a bloody mouth and confess to crimes both horrendous and false.

In the Gulag, people had been killed for less than failing in their duty to the State. Yuri recalled (suddenly Yuri again and not the mechanical flesh-and-bone creature that soullessly deposited humans into the cold wastes) that he and other soldiers had cruelly stripped another, prettier officer and put him in a prison uniform for bragging about his lovers. No one in high command had said a word when they saw the man, suddenly quartered with the enemies of the state, screaming at them that he was a good and loyal communist. They did not bat an eyebrow, nor even acknowledge his presence. It had only been a week before the pretty, experienced former officer was a corpse to be ferried in Yuri's truck, and Yuri had no particular mirth or glee when he dumped the body alongside the other prisoners in a sacrificial pile.

Now Yuri wanted to go back and die at the barrel of the gun rather than at the canine fangs of frostbite. He would rather become part of the unspeakable corpse foundation than be alone in the tundra. He gulped, started his truck and began to steer back towards the prison.

It was easy enough to navigate his return when he went on his grave-runs. He was not careless; he did not drive for hours or ever put himself in danger of running out of gas. He had no delusions; no one would look for him if he did not come back. A notice may be sent out, his face sent to various train stations and an execution order placed on his name in case he turned up anywhere he shouldn't, but no rescue party would be sent. More effort was put into the creation rather than recovery of corpses, and every hand was needed in the prisons.

This night, however, the frantic attempt to escape back south seemed to go on forever. He went for hours, looking desperately outside as the lights of the stars and moon became dimmer and the landscape began to glow like cadaverous, phosphorous fungus. Tonight there was something unusual in the snow, which became increasingly incandescent and bright as the night went darker and darker. The cab of the car became smaller with every moment, and beneath his layers of wool and fur Yuri could feel the damp chill of sweat sliding over him.

Something in him was about to explode. There was a sort of premonition and hyper-awareness that crawled along the wrinkles of his brain and whispered that something horrible was about to extend its claws into his bleeding heart. His teeth clamored as he heard a frantic throbbing not in his heart but in his head, veins pumping blood to his brain in an attempt to make him superhumanly alert.

Then the world went wrong.

There was a moment of deafening noise, the roar of a gigantic monster out in the darkness that rocked the car and sent Yuri into shocks of spinal tremors. The wind began to pick up and howl; slamming sheets of glowing snows against the truck. There was a scream in the wind, the oscillating cry of a cat with human lips being skinned with a rusted knife. Yuri panicked, about to scream Orthodox prayers that he had not uttered since he was a child. He cried out for his father when a shadow smashed against the windshield.

The glass cracked and shattered, as reality broke apart for a moment. The truck sputtered, cranked, and exploded into smoke in front of him. He could not see the thick fog that choked him, but felt the exhaust and smoke pour like poison into his lungs. He could taste the fire. Panic swelled up in him as he thrust the door of the truck open, ignoring any wounds he may have suffered in the crash. It did not occur to Yuri that in the tundra there was nothing to crash into.

The fatal frigid air was on him again.

He cried out, but the silence was gone, and could not hear himself over the pitch of the wind. The car was making a rattling noise, whining and squeaking like a little bird. Through the wind he could detect only the faintest hint of smoke. Blinking and near the point of nature-induced blindness, Yuri walked towards the front of his truck, aware that at any point it could explode. Any attempt on his part to understand or rationalize what had happened would calm him. Perhaps with a clearer mind, he could fix his vehicle and get back to the prison.

He tripped, falling face-forward onto the hard ice.

He was on top of something, something large and... *warm*. With a herculean effort, Yuri pushed himself off of the ice floor and shifted himself to crouch over the object that had tripped him. The ice was fighting him at every turn, the snow picking up more speed as its glowing white surface came to engulf the night. Yet it was because of this unnatural, strange snow-light that Yuri could clearly see the cause of his fall, but was unwilling to accept it at first.

Then he laughed.

It finally made sense!

He had tripped over one of his corpses, discarded from the truck by some bump that Yuri had been too drunk to detect. The bump, whatever it was, had somehow jostled the engine and radio. Salty tears came down his face and left burning streaks where they froze. He would have to look at the engine again. Hopefully he could fix it so he could get back. He thanked God that the radio was broken. His call to the Gulag, even if it had been an honest mistake, could have become a death sentence.

The snow stopped for a moment, the land seemed to revert back to its natural tranquility. Yuri saw the body in full form, and a glacial terror receded from his eyes all the way down the base of his spine. It was a man; his skin was a sanguine red, full of more blood than men were supposed to—especially dead men. He looked...*ripe*, a very *ripe* and red corpse that had let loose little streams of steam. There was not a patch of blue or black over the man, impossible since all starving prisoners died and decayed prematurely from the cold.

The man was unnaturally *healthy*.

He was lean, but not skeletal, with an uncharacteristic plumpness in his stomach; his closed eyes weren't hallowed cavities, but were, instead, normal and even handsome.. There was something oddly grotesque in the uncharacteristic *plumpness* of his stomach, the bulge resembled someone who had been fed well for a long period of time . There were no stomachs like that in the Gulag. The only fat that existed was in the trash-meat soup they fed the officers who watched over barbed-wire walls and ramshackle wooden mausoleums.

Yuri, not in courage but in that reflexive curiosity which makes children touch stoves, went to the body to stoop over it. He could not recognize the face or any other distinguishable thing about the body. There was nothing about the shape of the nose, the sculpting of the chin or any sort of scars or hair that would have caused Yuri to recognize the man. He was part of an endless, unremarkable crowd, only remarkable because he stood out against the decrepit wreckage of what is left in the human frame after its humanity has been forcefully removed.

The heat was radiating and vibrating in an invisible cloud. There was an *aura* of perverse warmth in the air next to the corpse—that unlike a fireplace this created no comfort. It was unnatural, musky and humid in a place where water was dry. Every nerve on Yuri was creeping, every inch of him humming with tense electricity as he reached down to touch the man's forehead.

He felt the heat through his glove.

The corpse's eyes opened.

This time Yuri heard his own scream. The eyes were glazed over and grey—the ornament-eyes of a troglodyte creature to which light is useless. Bulbous and blind though they were, Yuri could feel them following him as he ran away stupidly and desperately from the corpse and his truck. The eyes followed him like the bead of the gun, and Yuri felt that he was in a line of sight far more dangerous than any armed soldier.

The wind stirred up again, into a maelstrom of glowing white snow that blotted out the night. The storm was an assault on his senses, where sight became muddled with the booming cacophony of the blizzard and his sense of touch became as dull and blunted as his eyes. There was an undercurrent of exhaustion and electricity under Yuri's skin as his breathing became more ragged with each gasp. He moved slowly, encumbered by his clothing, and tripped over something again. Shivering, screaming, the reflexive realization rushed to Yuri's mind before his subconscious could try to repress it:

Warm.

Yuri could feel the tears and snot on his face, panic binding him as much as the storm around him. Yuri felt the softness of flesh through his glove as he lifted himself from the thing he could not see. His mind recited all the prayers he had ever been taught into incoherent syllables, streaming together chants and songs that he had forgotten until he needed them. Everything in him was alert, stumbling and crying through the blizzard. He fell over five times in what only seemed like a few minutes. Each time he felt the awful, steady warmth beneath him, and each time he pushed himself off of something other than hard ice.

The flurry must have masked the graveyard, the unholy place where corpses were still warm and opened their eyes to watch their gravedigger at his work. A creature seemed to scream out in the wind, a demonic laughing cry that came through the whipping white and the night blackness. It was not far from him, he imagined only a few yards away and getting closer with each shrill call that matched the tempo and torrent of the storm. The place was littered with these warm bodies, and he could feel the weight of their blind eyes laughing malevolently as he stumbled and tripped over them.

He was not a bad man! No worse than the men he worked with! But he had been a hero! He had been a hero of Stalingrad! Stalin had *personally* thanked him! This alone should have been a ticket for his salvation, *something* to save him from whatever cruel trick the winds and snow were playing on him now! He screamed out his life, that it was not his fault men were killed! He was not the one who decided to leave their corpses unhallowed in the Tundra; he was not the one who gave the order to pollute the Siberia with the litter of executions!

The wind lifted him off of the ground and tossed him onto another warm body. Screaming, thrashing against the loose arms that softly wrapped around him like a mother, Yuri pulled free and began running again. There was no destination in his mind, even if he had cleared his mind for a moment and thought rationally, the Gulag was no longer open to him.

The tundra had exposed itself to him, the casualties of war and cold had been revealed to Yuri and he knew he could never work in snow again. He would leave Siberia; he would run across the Arctic Circle into Canada. He would keep running until he never saw snow or ice again!

Something cold and strong grabbed at his ankle, pulling him down and dragging him along the endless floor. He clawed at the ground with all his force, making out red trails through the flurries and he knew that the blood was from his own raw, ungloved fingers. Death was all around him now, the storm thundering and mixing with the own songs and prayers in his head into a mocking sound. He flipped upright and exposed his cold throat.

Was he choking, or were there cold fingers thrusting themselves into his mouth? Was something laughing at him? Were there warm, red bodies standing around in snow looking down on him? They must have been, he could see them, smiling stupidly with straight white teeth, staring with lifeless grey eyes unmeant for sunlight.

The grey eyes were unchanging, constant and unmoving. They did not blink, but glinted and shifted with the patterns of shifting snow. He could not hear breath, moans or any other sounds to indicate the existence of sentience in those eyes. Only the patience, the constancy and weight of the stares crushed Yuri into believing that he was being watched. He was dying, he was mad and he was dying while the lifeless world watched without remorse.

The cold was inside of him now, his throat dry and cut with shards of ice and fear. An arm covered in knives was tearing him apart from the inside, and he could feel the taste of wind-scarred blood running down his mouth. Every part of him seemed to bleed as numbness spread from his fingers to his arms. Slowly all motion became impossible as his nerves became unresponsive. The numbness entered his lungs and crept into his heart.

A new, mad, thought entered into his head:

Breath, please, breath!

His lungs stopped heaving. The throbbing in his head soon became aware of the slowing of his heart, calming and stopping for intolerable intervals. All thought left him, and death entered Yuri Zaystev as one final, slithering breath.

The steam from Yuri's face rose up into the dark. The now calm air of the tundra night. The world around him watched content with another of countless bodies that had already been brought into its fold. Nothing blinked for centuries, and nothing changed for all eternity.

Yuri had been wrong in one regard: they had not sent a search party for him, but they sent one for his truck. After all, equipment was expensive and valuable. Yuri would be replaced after he was killed, and his replacement would drive his truck. The soldiers followed the tracks to a spot not far from the prison.

Yuri lay on the ground next to the truck, eyes frozen permanently open on a green-blue face with an open mouth.

His mouth seemed to have been forming a word when he died, but no mention was made of that in the report. Yuri's name disappeared into records, and his body was left to disappear into the unknowable currents and winds of the Tundra. He was never found or remembered again.

THE MARKED MEN

BEN STALLWOOD

I had a dream...

Dear Greta,

This letter must come as a shock. I'm sorry I couldn't find another way to contact you first. My name is Emily, and I deeply wish we had had the chance to meet in person before all this, not least because I feel like it would have made having to write this letter easier. As it is, this letter seems so impersonal and inappropriate that even as I write, I still don't know whether or not it will do you more harm than good. Please, please accept my sincerest assurance that any hurt caused by receiving this package is far removed from what I intended. However, I deeply feel, that these papers enclosed belong with you and your family, and not with mine. In the end, I suppose I feel that if it were my family that were the subject of these notes and not yours, I would like them returned to me, however much hurt they may cause. The last thing I wanted to do was to reopen old wounds.

I don't know whether or not Per ever mentioned me in connection to Dylan or whether Dylan himself ever told you about me. I'm not sure how often the boys would talk about things like their wives or children. I never met Per, although we spoke over the telephone on a few occasions when he called the house looking for Dylan. He seemed like an unbelievably gentle person.

Firstly, I just wanted to tell you how deeply, deeply sorry I am for your loss. I can't find the words to tell you how overcome I was when Dylan told me about the death of your son. It's not something that should ever have to happen. If there was anything I could do to help, even to share the pain, I would. There is nothing worse than the death of a young man, especially one as talented and imaginative as Yngve must evidently have been.

Secondly, by way of an explanation, I'm writing because Per sent me the letters enclosed in this package last June, and as I said, I feel that they are rightfully yours. I don't know why Per sent them to me. I knew that Dylan was writing a journal whilst away but I never read it until Per sent me these pages from it. It was always an issue of trust between us that I never interfered with his work until he invited me to; having read these now, I feel like I have somehow violated something between us. There's also material here written by Per himself, that relates to Yngve, that seems incredibly sensitive, and I don't feel that it is appropriate for me to keep this.

Again, I'm sorry that I had to send you such difficult and painful material in such an abrupt way. However, I really, strongly feel that I am doing the only thing that I can do by sending them back to you. I think Per thought that reading these would help me find some sort of solace, but all they have done is raised questions that have no answers, and left my mind in a kind of turmoil.

I've enclosed the letters below

✳ ✳ ✳

...a wondrous thing

It seem'd....

Dylan's Journal: 07/05/2011, mid-morning, on the plane

You can't ever really imagine the way a forest looks until you are there in it. What people fail to imagine is the detail. When people think about forests they think about something like a child's drawing; flat plains with straight, symmetrical trees growing at regular intervals like rows of posts. Once you are there, you realize it's nothing like that. It's chaos, without a straight line in sight. Everything you see is its own living be-ing, fighting for water and sunlight. Every tangle of thorns, bank of undergrowth, hollow and stump is a microcosm, like a continent on a tiny scale. Every tree is alive.

I love the woods. It's the smell that brings them to life, that really lets you know you're not just looking at a picture or watching TV, but are really there in the middle of it. You can nearly taste the leaf-mould; that damp scent like old houses where the moss is creeping I wish I could bottle it and bring it home with me. I'd sit at my desk and sniff it when I began to feel restless, the same way other people look at postcards.

But here, as well as the woods and the mountains, there's the water. That's what makes Norway so different to anywhere else in Europe. We are nearly in Bergen, and the plane has just banked to give me a view of one of the fjords. It's a huge, silver coil of water—so vast you could lose a whole city in it. I think we must be flying up the coast from the south. Perhaps it is Stavanger? I will ask Per when I see him.

If the woods seem like countries and continents then the water is the sky, and space—massive, blank and unreadable. And the rock is jagged and tumbling, and huge, the way that an adult looks to a tiny child. I can't describe it. I don't have the skill.

The landscape here sets my imagination racing. Flying into Bergen, I always get the same feeling. I feel like a little kid. Grown-ups aren't supposed to think about things like trolls in the woods and the *Jotun* throwing boulders off the cliffs. I try and rationalize it to myself—my adult self—by pretending it's serious and historic and not just fun and fantastical. I imagine Norwegians a thousand years ago sailing longships down the fjords out into the open sea, seeing the cliffs and the water all around them, and inventing these monsters to express their fear and explain the world. Then I daydream. Vikings are just as much a fantasy as the trolls, in this day and age.

But really, that's why I'm writing this. I always come on these trips so exuberant, full of these crazy thoughts that I feel like a different person to the Dylan behind his desk in London. It's so hard to keep these ideas to myself. I have to express it somehow or else I'll end up ranting to the flight attendants about Eric the Red, and they'll probably think I'm drunk. I can't talk to Per about it, either. He's good company, Per, really he is, but he's so cynical and hard about it all. He just sees all of this as something for the tourists. Besides, he sees the countryside here every day. He's used to it, and he's very much a part of the 'modern Norway'—sharp suits, speaks four languages, loves Portuguese food. If I'm honest, I find it a little bit disappointing. He's not the type of person I could start going on about trolls to.

The seatbelt sign has just come on. I think we're landing. If I don't let the excitement out I feel like I'll burst. I can't wait to smell the woods again.

✳ ✳ ✳

Dylan's Journal: 07/05/2011, Afternoon, in the taxi

We landed safely. Bergen airport is sort of wheel-shaped from above. It's a classic piece of Nordic design—unashamedly efficient and sort of knowingly weird. I remember Per's wife Greta, a Swede, showing me around the Lipstick building in

Gothenburg one year —"A classic piece of dorky Scandinavia," as she put it. The Norwegians are the same as the Swedes, really. Everything feels slightly 'ironic,' although I'm sure Per and Greta would stickle with me over that point.

Per has given me the address to the campsite that he says I need to give to the bus driver, because he doesn't trust me to pronounce Norwegian names. I'm not going there straight away, though. I'm spending my first night here in Bergen, so I've taken a taxi to Bergen city centre. I've asked him to take me to the Bryggen district, by the harbour.

I've known Per for ten years. We used to meet twice yearly; us, Naotake, Wyatt and the others on the *Photovolt* project. Most of the work was done via Skype, of course, but every so often we'd all conspire together and come up with some excuse, about how the funding panel absolutely *had* to send us to Toronto or Bergen or Tokyo for some reason or other. It was always a great trip.

It was a weird mix of personalities, that group. Naotake I never got to know; I mean I knew him well but I never got to know *him* away from his nationality. Something always got lost in translation. It's not that his English wasn't good (and much better than my Japanese, of course) but it was hard to get a sense of him as anything more than a representative of his culture. He'd typically start conversations with things like 'In Asian culture', or 'speaking as a Japanese man', or something. Perhaps that was all he wanted.

Now I think about it, Per and Wyatt never quite understood each other. Wyatt, the Canadian, is one of the biggest idealists I've ever met. He's a real ideas-man as well. He would throw out suggestions and just sort of *jam* off the ideas. It didn't matter to him. It was all about the creation. He was a real artist, in a way, and he never lost sight of the politics behind sustainable design, either. He was really passionate. He saw himself as someone who was building the future.

I remember lying down on a roof terrace in Toronto with Wyatt, late at night, after having one too many beers, and Wyatt turned to me and said "Dylan, man, you know what the thing about this job is? We're a voice to the voiceless." I asked him what he meant and he told me that people who had no idea who we were were benefitting from our work. Photovolt, if it had caught on, would have saved fossil fuels and made electric cars a genuinely viable, affordable alternative to petrol. They could have spread around the world and the environmental impact would have had an influence globally, even to those people who would never drive the Photovolt cars. As petrol became scarce, Photovolt would have become the cheaper option in disadvantaged countries. It was sustainability for everyone, not just for a trendy few in Europe or the USA. And of course, the global affect on the environment would have much more of a beneficial impact in the developing world than in the west. It was about empowering people to change their own futures, not just waiting for us to do it for them. Wyatt had a real world vision.

Per was more pragmatic. Not even that, but in conversation. Per sat back one evening, smiling, and told us all that he had just sold his house for nearly twice what he had bought for it. I couldn't tell if he was joking or not. That was conversation, with Per. He was like a caricature of the kind of 'straight' that you didn't really find in the world of sustainable engineering. And that wound Wyatt up the wrong way. Wyatt could never quite figure Per out, either. There was always something... not *knowing*, exactly, but as if he had a point to prove to us all. He was always sharp and business savvy, but it always seemed like there was a whole other side to him at home, which he was quite happy for us not to see.

I think I hit it off with Per better than the others did. He had a family. He was very much a 2.4 kids kind of guy, which I found really sweet and endearing. That was what I think he thought us Anglophones would expect of him, to be more British than the British, and he didn't seem to mind playing up to it. As a design engineer he was fantastic, really technically knowledgeable, but quite (small-c) conservative. He could be quite negative at times, as well. He had a habit of 'blocking' a lot of Wyatt's ideas with small-scale practicalities and nit picking

Still, though, I don't want to criticise. It is Per that I am in touch with to this day, not Wyatt. He likes the outdoors just as much as I do. That's what matters.

Per's son died in November. I'm not sure exactly what happened. I didn't want to ask. It seems inappropriate, somehow, just to dwell on the gory details. I know it was quite sudden. I can't imagine anything worse.

I haven't spoken about it to Per, but I insisted that we'd do our walking holiday this spring, like always. I don't know whether he'll want to talk, or not. I don't know how deeply ingrained that Scandinavian stiff-upper-lip has become.

Back to the taxi ride—we're about twenty minutes out of the airport and just coming into Bergen itself. The driver is a proper local. Very gruff and Nordic. A real character. He'd probably be quite trendy in London at the moment, with his big beard and Christmas jumper all year round. I'm considering telling him.

We're heading east. I can see the forest on either side, above the Bergen suburbs. I'm always fascinated by how landscapes and living interact. I love the way the industrial buildings nestle here amongst the boulders and mountains. The trees are green and gold in the sun, and between the trunks I can see flashes of dazzling water. I'm so excited.

Dylan's Journal: 07/05/11, Evening, Bergen Sentrum

I flew out a day early and I'm not meeting Per until tomorrow. I wanted a night to myself in Bergen first. I love this city. The fjord, the harbour and the mountains shape the landscape of the city like the canals in Venice do. In fact, that's what Bergen most reminds me of: A Nordic Venice. From the city centre, Bergen looks like a tiny village. The mountains around the harbour are steep, sparsely populated with little wooden cottages, and undeveloped and densely forested at the peaks, even within walking distance of the city centre. The houses rise up about five or six deep and then peter out into what looks like wilderness. It's a city developed with a mind for nature,

I think, or possibly just for tradition. The big industrial and population centres are out of sight, behind the mountains. I know it's a UNESCO heritage city, so possibly there are laws in place about what can and can't be built within sight of the old town.

I'm staying at the YMCA, a street away from the harbourside fish market and the stall that sells reindeer hides that always seems to be there whenever I visit. I haven't stayed in a dormitory since my gap year. I remember a few older travellers then, but now I feel a little self-conscious to be sharing a room with all these cool young things. I suppose times have changed.

I'm sat writing this by the harbour. Speedboats are criss-crossing the water. Out in the harbour mouth, in the distance, a few huge tankers are looming in over the smaller boats like parents watching their kids running around. It was hot today, like an English summer, but now the sun has begun to set (at just after midnight!) you can feel the cold air coming from the harbour and it chills under the skin, and you remember just how far north you really are. I think about the arctic water under my feet, imagine it lapping over my skin, icecap cold.

Dylan's journal: 08/05/11, Morning, on the bus.

I used to think Norway didn't have a smell at all. Even the forests themselves smell clean, efficient and Scandinavian, but that's partly to do with the sheer content of water and the strong winds. There's a slight salt smell—crisp, and slightly bitter. The main body of trees are coniferous. They're either fir or pine but I don't know the difference. I'm so used to the pine air-fresheners we have at home that walking into the woods almost feels like going indoors.

The forests around Bergen seem sort of tame. Mount Ulvik is like a child's drawing of a mountain. It's nearly triangular, sheer-sided in comparison to the flat harbour basin, as if someone had just put it there. The other mountains around Bergen are similar. They're pointed triangles, like the picture on a Toblerone packet. I can't wait to get out into the proper wild.

I caught the tram to somewhere a little bit suburban-feeling (although still at the foot of a mountain, naturally) and then got on a bus from there. Per has told me the driver will take me straight to the campsite to meet him. We'll spend tonight at the campsite, and then tomorrow a car will meet us and drive us north to the start of the trail.

The road follows the edge of a fjord. I watch the sea stretch away between the angular peaks. Ahead of us, the fjord peters out into a flat, forested basin that seems to glisten with surface water like a marsh, although whether this is an island or a delta I can't tell at first. When I get closer I realise that the water has been forced into a channel through the boggy basin; a narrow bottle-neck of what seems to be fresh water, speckled with massive, cartoon-style lily pads. Beyond this channel is a fresh water lake, a few miles across. I look back, and suddenly the salt-water fjord behind me looks vast and bleak by comparison to the little lake. The bus window is open, and I'm beginning to shiver. The wind coming in is bitter with salt. Together the ocean and the mountains fade into the mist.

A little sickness in the air...

* * *

Diary

If found, please return to _____

I don't want to write anything.

I don't want to

This is ~~stupid~~ pointless

I'm waiting for Dylan, and I'm thinking about Yngve. My therapist told me to write things down to express myself. I've read the studies and it's a sound theory, although under-evidenced, like so much of this person-centred psychology is, but I can't help feeling like the practical application here was a little over-zealous. There, now I'm writing. The therapist's suggestion left me feeling angry, and patronized, as I left the clinic clutching this little notebook to myself. It was as if someone had tried to stick a plaster over an amputation. I'm not an expert, but I don't think that's the aim of the exercise. I'd rather someone gave me pills.

Is that what you wanted?

I'm supposed to write every time I think about Yngve. Well, I'm writing now. Not because I'm thinking about him, but because I can feel him. His presence is here even though he's not consciously in my thoughts. What I am thinking about is my new hiking boots, Google Maps on my phone, how much water we will need to bring, and whether or not I can get Dylan to carry the tent, but what I am feeling is melancholy, in spite of the trip we've got planned, and it has to be Yngve that's making me feel like that. Why am I thinking about Yngve? It started as soon as I opened the car window on the trip out of Voss, and smelled the woods in spring; I suppose it's nostalgia. Yngve used to play in the woods as a kid.

It's the smell that brings it all back. It smells dusty, and sweet and rotten. You can see nature on the TV and it's just so many moving colours, but it's the smell that tells you that you are really there. Dylan says the same thing, every time we come here, and this time it will cut me up to hear him say it because he knows it, but he doesn't understand what that means to me. It's the smell that brings back my loss. Just for an instant, the feeling is so strong that it makes my knees buckle and I choke back tears.

So, I'm just going to write. Later, someone can read all this and try and put the pieces together. Maybe I have a nightmare every time I see someone wearing blue, or something. That's the problem with the subconscious; you need a professional to read it for you. Not very *person-centred*, is it?

I'm starting to enjoy writing this, now. I'm stood at the gate of the campsite, leaning this notebook on the gatepost.

It's a round wooden stake the width of the spread of my hand. Underneath my notepad, the wood is crumbling away like it's been gouged out. There is dry moss peeling away like scabs. The wood underneath the moss is a lighter shade than the rest of the post, and smooth.

There's a track down to the campsite. About fifteen miles away is the main E-road out of Bergen. Dylan will be coming down the track soon, with that big stupid grin on his face and all these reductive little comments about 'Scandinavia' and how quiet and empty and quaint it all is. I'm going stand here in the woods with my wireless headphones and watch *The Thick Of It* on my iPad, or read *Wolf Hall* on my Kindle, or something, and maybe I can make my own little assumptive remarks about 'Britishness' as well. He'll love that. I can speak his language better than he does.

So the campsite... There's a clearing in the woods and a small, rocky beach that stretches down towards a lake. There's a row of log cabins on the shore of the water, and a jetty with rowing boats tethered to it. There's several incredibly expensive, silver, American-style camper vans, the size of yachts, with Danish or German or Dutch licence plates. We're staying in the cabin tonight, and probably drinking, and maybe getting a boat out onto the water so Dylan can look at the late-night sunset.

I'm being unfair on Dylan, but I'm not looking forward to seeing him. I know he'll try and talk to me about Yngve. If he doesn't, I'll spend the whole trip waiting for him to. I feel almost nervous, waiting for him. I'm so tired of talking about

Yngve. I never even talked about him this much when he was alive. My therapist told me that she understood what I was feeling because her mother died when she was a teenager, although she didn't say it in so many words. Part of me thought that that doesn't count. I'm angry all the time at the moment. Even in the woods, I feel bitter. I'd get angry with the trees if I had an excuse to. I'm frustrated, as if things are crawling on me. I didn't want to come along on this stupid trip. It was arrogant of Dylan to make me. That's why I'm pissed at him really.

At the edge of the water, there are thick fronds of bracken and tall grass growing nearly to my waist. The greenery is thicker and richer this year than ever before; great explosions of wet, glistening bracken burst from the undergrowth like frozen fountains. I find it slightly unsettling, these unnatural displays of fertility, distorted to the extreme, like women with oversized, fake breasts.

People talk about brain sicknesses, like Yngve's, as if they were actual diseases, and this is useful because it helps alleviate blame from the individual. Simply put, they can't help cutting themselves or shooting themselves any more than people can help sneezing or having diarrhoea. But when Yngve died I was so angry with him I felt like having him thrown into the sea.

Yngve cut his wrists a lot, but the first time I think he tried to kill himself was two years ago when he tried to drown himself in the fjord at Arna under the shopping centre. I heard the door close in the night. Yngve slammed it so loudly that I knew he wanted me to follow him, to try and stop him. I stayed in bed because I was sick of his stunts by that stage.

He had a bike lock with him

The police phoned me and brought him home about 5 in the morning. They said he'd been stood by the water's edge, in the horseshoe ring of mountains, just behind the petrol station opposite Arna bus terminal. He'd just been stood there looking out at the water, watching all the big boats drifting around in the misty distance. The police searched him, because he was stoned, and found his backpack was filled up with bricks, and then one of the police looked out into the harbour, looked down in between the little speedboats moored at the jetty and realized why Yngve had a backpack full of bricks.

He was going to fix the bike lock around the two straps and fasten it across his chest so that he couldn't take the bag of bricks off his back once he was in the fjord, and then jump in—I mean, that was the idea. I'm not sure whether at that stage he would have gone through with it or not. It was like he knew he didn't want to die. Why else would he have to lock the bag onto his back? I thought it was like he had to make himself die somehow, to prove a point or as some sort of punishment or because he thought he should.

Yngve was beaten up in school once and was taken to hospital and he was clinically dead for a minute or so. He told Greta once he thought he was still dead. It was like a preoccupation of his. One day I was cooking on the hob and Yngve walked right past me like he didn't even see I was there and put his hands in the flame.

In one sense it was like a sickness in that there was a long decline, and gradually Yngve dying began to feel inevitable.

But again, it's about blame. We started to imagine an irrevers-ible, terminal deterioration because we couldn't see what we ourselves could do to reverse it. I don't believe you can cure people like that. Yngve wanted to die too badly.

As I walk'd in a stilly wood...

Dylan's Journal: 09/05/2011, Early morning, camp site, by the lake

The woods are ancient and rotting. The water is massive, blank and unreadable. The rock is jagged and tumbling, and huge, the way a parent looks to a tiny child.

Oh god, Per's done it again. I realized why we've been friends for so long now. As much as he plays this hard-nose cynic, I know he has a romantic side for nature in the same way that I do. This spot he has picked is perfect. I'm stood here now, waiting for the taxi to pick us up, unable to take my eyes off the scenery and gawping like a kid in a toyshop. The campsite is on the shore of the lake that I saw from the bus yesterday morning. The lake is utterly still and as clear as a mirror, and the mountain at the far side is ridged with three great big glacial gouges out of it. It looks like a clenched fist, pulling the flat shimmer of the lake and the valley taut. There are children swimming; tiny figures in the vast, flat, cold water, and there is a forested island that seems like a mile away in comparison. The jetty stretches out into the water like a finger, pointing. And the huge, squat peak on the far side is reflected in the water as an exact double. But beyond the lake is the fjord; I can't see it but I can feel its presence. This is hard to explain, but the fjord seems to represent a concept that has been forming in my mind as much as a physical thing—the idea of 'North.' There's an occasional cold wind that suddenly howls out of nowhere, although there are no clouds in the sky, and chases away the still, hazy late spring air.

I met Per here at the campsite yesterday afternoon. God, he looks bad. He's thin, and looks like he's not sleeping at night. We hugged, a little awkwardly. I'm sure he noticed the surprise on my face.

Last night we stayed at the campsite, in a cabin, which Per had hired out—very quaint. I'm sure 'Log Cabin, Norway' holds enough visual connotations as a phrase that I don't need to describe it. It was just as you'd imagine, even painted red with little yellow window frames.

It was a strange evening, sort of awkward. I don't know whether this is because of what's happened to Per, or because meetings between old friends who haven't seen much of each other often are a little awkward at first. Per was quiet most of the evening, and just as I was thinking of going to bed he suddenly, out of the blue, suggested that we should take one of the rowing boats out into the river. It was quite a strange suggestion, and Per seemed so keen to do so that there was almost a hint of desperation about him. I told him I wanted to get an early night so we could be off early today. I'm glad I did now; I'm glad I'm not too tired and hung over to appreciate this.

The camp site is roughly four hour's drive south from the start of our trek, and then thirty mile's hike from there to the fjord that will eventually be our base camp for the next week. Per said we would make the trip over two days. He said he chose a spot where we can pitch our tent overnight, roughly half way to the fjord. At the campsite, now, waiting for the car, I feel like I'm at the last bastion of civilization on the edge of a frontier. Norway's a huge, empty country. Even to me, thirty miles seems like a long way. We'll be thirty miles away from the nearest other humans, most likely. This is exactly what I was hoping for, being able to walk for days and see no signs that humans were ever here. Wilderness like this doesn't really exist in the UK. This is why I come here every year.

I woke up in the night, as well. I'd forgotten about these northern nights. I woke up at about two in the morning and for a moment I was completely disoriented. It wasn't fully dark, there was just this grey, twilight glow throwing long, dark shadows across the cabin from the western horizon. At least, I assume it must be west. It's hard to tell when you're so far north.

There was this noise, a sort of croaking sound. It took me a while to persuade myself to get out of bed. I just lay there, looking at the light and listening to this noise. It would be silent, and as I was falling asleep I would hear it again. When I looked out of the window there was a fox sat on the window-sill. It looked thin, and small, but then I'm never sure how big foxes are supposed to be. It was staring through the glass at something on the far wall of the cabin, behind the bed.

Dylan's Journal: 09/05/2011, Afternoon, the first peak

The road north from the campsite was empty. I think by car is not the best way to see Norway. It's hard to get much of a sense of the landscape through the thick trees and sheer rock faces that hem in the mountain roads. You can't see much except the odd flash of blue-grey water through the gaps in the rock. The driver hardly spoke as he unpacked our bags and left us, in the middle of nowhere. I think he thought we were crazy.

That image of our first sight of the wilderness will always stay with me; the driver left us on what must have been a plateau. We had seen nothing but trees for miles, and suddenly we found ourselves on this bare stretch of what could almost have been a cold desert; grey-green, dry and littered with rocks. The mountains are much higher and craggier here than in Bergen, but we seem to be above the peaks. You can imagine people living amongst the highlands here for years and never knowing what's in the next valley. In the distance, the peaks are snow-capped. We begin our trek by heading northwards and down, in the direction of the flowing water, back into the tree cover.

The first leg of the hike was through the forested valley on the north side of the plateau, and then up over the low ridge of the next mountain in front of us. I didn't mind the steep climb down and back up. It was such a good feeling to finally be there. I hadn't realized how much I'd been champing at the bit to be let loose here until I finally felt the first slither of earth under my boots. The scramble on the slopes was fun. The winding paths and the way in which the rain (Per tells me it has rained a lot so far this spring) had obviously changed the shape of the hillside by washing away the soil from the rock, made the hike seem a little bit more adventurous. There are slabs of bare stone jutting out of the undergrowth, and great deposits of black earth around the roots of trees.

Per is still quiet, and we walked in relative silence, but then that's not altogether unusual. The woods are the focus, here. For Per it's the challenge, all that Ray Mears survival stuff. For me, it's about creativity, and letting my imagination flow.

Even so, I imagine he must be thinking about his son. I try not to feel awkward. I've told myself the worst thing I can do is feel awkward, to treat Per any differently than I normally would. He doesn't need that.

The climb was, I think, steeper than Per had imagined when he planned the route, and in places the slope became a little precarious. We had to switch between the narrow paths on a few occasions, where rock slides or fallen trees or rain had made them impassable, and we had to pick our way through the undergrowth to the next strip of empty ground with enough little rocks to use as footholds. Still, this is real woodland, not a park. There is no reason why the path should have been maintained for walking use. I prefer it this way. I like to imagine we are the first people to have climbed here for years. Between the paths, the undergrowth has grown so high it nearly smothers you. I have nettle stings on my neck.

We reached the peak after about five hours (I can't see the point of keeping an exact track of time, although Per no doubt does) and have sat down now on some boulders for a break. From a clearing on the summit looking south I can faintly see the plateau of the mountain where we were dropped off, and the dim line of the road. North, I can see the forest and more mountains and the endless, marbled veins of bright water stretching away until they merged with the sky in a blue-green haze. The trees are like a green ocean, stretching away to the horizon. Just past this peak is a wide, sweeping valley and another ridge, higher than this one and broken twice in the middle so that it looks like three enormous vertebrae on a gnarled old spine. Beyond this ridge is the fjord that we are going to, although it is still out of sight

Directly beneath me, as I look forward and down the steep slope, great thick walls of undergrowth rise towards me like surging waves. Fallen trees flounder in a sea of nettles and long, white-tipped grass, their branches arching over the undergrowth like they're waving for help, all under a canopy that taints the colour of the light, like bottle glass.

Per tried to focus my attention on the path we would be taking, on the slope directly in front of us, but I felt my gaze drawn incessantly outwards, north, towards the endless wilderness. Then suddenly, I looked downwards past my feet and I imagined myself falling. The bottom of the valley must be miles down. I could feel the rush of cold air, and imagine the touch of every one of a hundred thousand leaves and branches as I plummeted down the mountainside.

I am sat at the peak, writing. We've only allowed ourselves an hour's respite to see the view and I'm conscious that we need to press on again. The time doesn't matter so much, it never really gets dark here, but we need to reach a place to camp while we still have enough energy left to pitch the tent. Looking out again, the feeling of size, space and vertigo is so intoxicating that I feel almost sick. Per is complaining about the amount of water that we've brought, but I am finding it hard to focus on what he is saying.

Overhead, not out over the valley, but directly above the peak, directly above us, a bird of prey is circling. It is beautiful, although I can only see its silhouette. It wheels in a circle, catches wind, changes direction suddenly and then continues its slow arc above us, apparently endlessly.

...hollow, lush and damp

Dylan's Journal: 09/05/2011, Nighttime

It's nighttime now, although still light. We made camp in the valley. I'm exhausted. Rather than climb straight down the mountain we had to work our way along the ridge in search of a safe path, which, I must admit, I found a little frustrating, especially after we had sat there for so long doing nothing. By the time we made camp I'd almost stopped taking in my surroundings at all and was having to focus instead on walking, putting one foot in front of the other. The difficult paths became harder to navigate as the day went on and I grew wearier.

It was stinking hot in the woods. I've never seen the forest this green before—the deciduous trees seemed to sag under the weight of their own foliage. I remember the green spilling forward, great, heavy tendrils hanging from every branch, so much of it that it almost hurts your eyes to look at.

The tree cover absorbed the heat, but deflected the drying rays of the sun itself. The woods were not only hot but damp, too, from the water in the trees and on the undergrowth. I could almost imagine the water in the trunks steaming away, turning the woods into some kind of primordial sauna. I couldn't take off my jacket because of the straps in my backpack. I was sweating so much I dropped my water bottle. I remember I couldn't tell which of the lumps sticking to my sweaty skin were insects crawling on me and which were solid matter from my own pores. It stank, too. The smell of the undergrowth is sharp, like ammonia.

The sun is beginning to set, at last. I can feel the cold night air on my face as if I could drink it in through my skin—although, of course, the sun won't actually set. The light streaks through the canopy as if through stained glass. The pools of sunshine on the rotten floor are bright, deep orange like fire. Occasionally a streak of light will break through and dazzle an entire section of the path, and then, momentarily, it is like the woods are ablaze.

Something really strange happened this evening too. We were nearing the spot that Per had chosen to camp in; it's an old logging clearing, apparently, but the track has long since grown over. As we drew closer, I began to hear a buzzing noise that sounded almost mechanical. It got louder and louder, not one sound but hundreds like distant traffic, except I had seen the view of the place from the ridge and I knew there were no roads for miles around.

When I broke through the tree cover and into the clearing, the ground was black and just for a moment I felt something stick in my throat. The forest floor was alive, coated with little, furry black bodies of these enormous, fat flies. I could see them, mounds of moving bodies climbing over one another, a writhing mass, until Per stepped forward and the carpet of flies suddenly rose into the sky like some huge, black mushroom cloud. I remember Per staggering back, covering his eyes and mouth, as the cloud briefly engulfed him and then flew up, and past, and dispersed into the sky.

It's a truly bizarre phenomenon. I've never seen anything like it. I think perhaps the flies need the direct sunlight in the clearing for warmth, or to feed, or something, so they gather there, but to see so many at once was quite a surprise. The clearing itself is about thirty feet across, flat, and a little boggy under foot. There is tall, brownish grass and nettles roughly to the height of our ribs, which we have flattened and hacked out in order to pitch the tent and make enough space around for us to sit, cook, and eat. Beneath the grass and nettles are deposits of sand, as well as the soil, which I think must have been to do with the logging once upon a time. The ground is drier on the sand than the soil.

I'm sat on a log, scratching away at this journal while Per

silently reads the GPS on his phone. I keep spitting midges out of my mouth.

He seem'd a dismal, murky stamp

I miss my son. It shouldn't be so hard to say, but it is. He was so unbelievably... *quiet*. I remember we'd hear music coming from his bedroom and see his shoes by the stairs, but other than that we wouldn't know if he was in the house or not for days at a time.

I remember walking into his bedroom once when he was eleven years old. He was sat on his bed, staring at the backs of his own hands and apparently doing nothing. When he saw me he screamed, and told me to fuck off. I was so shocked I didn't even punish him. I didn't know what to do. It became a joke, eventually. Leave Yngve alone. At home, the bedroom door is still closed. Greta won't go to the top floor of the house because it means walking past that big, silent, empty door and thinking that he's still there on the other side, locked in like he always was, ready to scream if we open the door. One day, I would like to go and kick that fucking door right down.

I never should have been a parent. I remember when Greta was pregnant, and I came home from work and there was no food in the house, and I made her dinner and she refused to eat it and told me it was horrible, and then she cried. I imagined ten years down the line, a kitchen table with Greta and four children all refusing to eat, and me so tired that I could barely speak, and I remember thinking *I don't want to have any children. I don't want them to end up like you.* How terrible a thought that is.

But I was an appalling parent, too. One day in the park some older children threw water balloons at Yngve. I picked him up and we left the park. He never mentioned it again and I never brought it up because I felt too ashamed of myself for not confronting the kids. He was so disappointed in me he wouldn't speak to me for the rest of the day. I could never set an example for him to follow. I could never be anything for him to aspire to.

I was never... I was negative, and indecisive. Greta stood and screamed at me about three weeks before our wedding, because I didn't seem excited, and I turned around and said to her 'well, you're the one who wants to get married.' Yngve never had a chance, being born into that kind of family.

Yngve came home from school every day for a week with a thick purple smear on his cheek where some kids had got handfuls of blackberries and rubbed them on his face. I tried to ask him about it and he threw a glass at the wall and went to his room. He sat in his room in the evenings until late. He wouldn't wash the purple juice on his face. He would come downstairs in the morning and it would have dried into a blue-black crust and he went to school with it still on his face, like...

I don't know what like. Like he wanted the kids to think

he didn't care, maybe? Or to see what they'd done? Or maybe just to upset us?

Another time a boy from Yngve's school spat on him in the street.

One time we had to go out in the evening on a week day to the late night shopping mall to buy him a new backpack because someone had put his old backpack in the toilet. I tried to make the trip fun, being out late on a weekday, all of that, and Yngve looked at me like he'd begun to hate me right then and there. That's what I remember as the turning point. That, to me, was the start of Yngve's sickness.

I know Yngve was difficult, but it was complicated. Trying to talk to him, to bring him out of himself, was this delicate and difficult art that Greta and I had been working on for years. We were nearly there. There were times when he was OK, for a year or so. He'd talk to us about stuff sometimes—we were fixing him, slowly, we thought, it just needed time. I can't help feeling like the kids in his school who used to bully him just did it for no reason at all. They pissed all over everything good we had, and killed my son and wrecked my life, for no reason.

His charnelhouse-grate...

I had a nightmare that there were things in the woods. I woke up and they still seemed to be there. I heard them last night. I tried to wake Dylan, but he wouldn't wake up. I could hear them—these bizarre, lifeless growls and the shuffles and thuds of legs that sounded crippled. Then I heard a gunshot, right above the tent. So close it sounded like it was coming from inside my skull, loud like something beating down on my head. I heard this gurgling sound like a bleeding throat outside and I felt my own jaw shudder as if it'd been ripped off.

When I woke up the outside of the tent was alive with black flies crawling over each other and trying to get in. Scores of them were inside already, thickening the air and beginning to cover Dylan and myself while we slept. I screamed, and they flew away. I can still feel them touching me.

With coffin-black, he barr'd the green

Dear mum and dad,

You'll be wondering why I did this. To be honest, I'm sorry to disappoint you, it was mainly about music. That and blood. Black Metal and Racial Pride are the only things that I really care about. This world is increasingly devoid of either and I don't want to be part of it anymore.

You need to understand. Black Metal music is synonymous with European racial identity but, like all

Aryan culture, it's a culture that is quickly being diluted and lost. Black metal music was never supposed to be for a mass market. People say it's elitist; well, yes it is. It's not for anyone to just go and buy a record.

I want to die because I hate Death Metal. I don't want to hear another Death Metal song. Death Metal is the watered down, commercialized form of Black metal. All I hear these days is Death Metal and I can't cope with it any more. I have to die. There's no other way.

Why do I hate Death Metal so much? That brings be onto my next point: Blood. I find it tragically ironic now that so many white, Scandinavian, supposedly 'Black Metal' bands have gone to Death Metal and have signed to Jewish-owned record labels in the process. The whole metal scene has allowed itself to fall under this kind of pervasive, Judeo-Liberal numbness that European culture has found itself being sucked into. Major record labels are just another ideological weapon to perpetuate this Judeo-Christian, Diet Cola, democratic dollar-cage, and blood is being diluted in the process.

I saw a kid today on the train wearing a t-shirt of the band Thorns. God, I wish I could have murdered that fucking poser. I hate this world where the rich fucking Jews can buy what isn't theirs, what is white by blood, that is nothing to do with them or with Jewry, and sell it to Americans and Africans and make money out of it, and no-one is prepared to stop them. I saw a poster for a tour rap music artists from Germany that was called the 'Midgard' tour. Why is it acceptable for non-Europeans to use European heritage as if it were their own culture? I would not expect a white band like Satanic Warmaster to name an album after Haile Selassie, or to hear Muslims talk about the Earl Mohammed or hear stories of the exploits of Samurai Svantevit, so why do these blacks and Jews think it's OK to take what's not theirs? Why do the liberal government let them get away with it? It's trivialising, and insulting. This is not a world that I want to live in.

I feel that the kind of democratic, commerce-based ideologies like Liberalism and Socialism, to which Mum and Dad subscribe, have allowed for our race to destroy its ancient culture and adulterate it's blood into something diluted, something more palatable and marketable to the mongrel masses. Weak humans are poisoning our race. Most of humanity is intellectually inferior to true Aryans anyway; most people I meet are reactionary, acting like a group of monkeys flinging its faeces at the wall every time its Liberal ideology is challenged. These lesser mind forms have pooled together and created a sort of 'lowest common denominator' which can be exploited by Judeo-Capitalist or Christian manipulators for the destruction of Norse, Gnostic, Pagan or Aryan language, culture and genetics. Black Metal was supposed to be the antithesis of this, a form of musical protest to accompany the kind of armed resistance that some of its brighter stars have perpetuated, but now it's more Happy Meal shit.

Anyway, what's my point? I want to die. Sorry if you thought this letter would be somehow deeper, would have more about you in it, Mum and Dad, but I don't actually give a fuck about you. You're probably thinking you failed as parents. You did, but that's not the point. I wanted to die a martyr.

Sorry about the mess. I know a shotgun is a fucking coward's way to die, and I dread to think what the pieces of my head are going to do the bedroom walls. I did try to cut my throat, but the knife was too blunt, and after that there was too much blood on my hands to hold it steady and make a proper incision on my wrists, so the gun was the only option. I've been practising with the shotgun in the woods anyway, shooting at people carved into trees. I think it's important for the white race to keep up its links to its warrior heritage by staying proficient with weaponry. After all, the Zog government won't defend us. And besides, I like the feeling of recoil.

So, Mum and Dad, you probably know more about me now than you ever have done. Be sure to bury me deep, and face down, lest I rise from my own fucking grave.

Blood and Honour.

Goodbye,

Yngve

THE MARKED MEN

* * *

"Death", said I, "What do you here?"

Dylan's Journal: 10/05/2011, Morning, leaving the camp site

It's morning. I didn't get a lot of sleep and I'm tired as a result, which is frustrating because we have a lot of ground to cover today. I wanted to be able to soak up the atmosphere and enjoy myself on the walk, whereas now I feel like it will be more of a test of endurance than anything else.

Per was awake most of the night, with the light from his phone on, writing in his notepad. We're sharing a two-man tent, and he kept us both awake. I can't help but feel like it was a little bit inconsiderate of him. I think he thought I was asleep.

We've just 'broken camp,' as it were. I'm sat on my rucksack writing this while Per is using the Google Maps app on his phone to try and find us a route. I think I preferred all of this when it was a bit less hi-tec. I was constantly trying to get this across on the design board for Photovolt—we needed to come up with ideas that were simple enough that local people could afford to maintain it, not just have to buy a new one every year. Otherwise, sustainability goes out of the window and we just become another unethical brand name. Besides that, Per's techno-stuff spoils the ambiance. There's so much beauty in these Scandinavian forests. I don't know how Per can stand to just stare at his screen all day.

I found something this morning. We were packing up the tent and underneath it, on the flattened grass, laid this thing. It's made out of twigs, tied together with some sort of metal wire that's rusted and started to dye the wood underneath it a reddish colour. There are four twigs in total: two forming a sort of crude crucifix shape and the other two, which are shorter, intersecting at either end of the crosspiece.

I don't know how we didn't see it last night when we were flattening the grass down. It was right underneath where we were sleeping. I'm not sure quite what it is about it, but I find it completely transfixing. It seems to me to represent a human form, or, from the other way up, a tree, or some amalgamation of these two entities: man and nature. There's just something captivating about the style in which it's made; that raw, lo-fi folk-art style that puts me in mind of something utterly ancient, especially because of the subject. People must have made models like these tens of thousands of years ago. It's the root of all art, in a way. Humanity's attempt to recreate its own image, to come to terms with itself, at the very dawn of human self-awareness. This must have been made and left here by the loggers. It's just really poignant; that same unconscious need for identity and self-analysis felt throughout history, still felt today by ordinary working-class people the world over, when faced with the wilderness. It's made of wood, and tree shaped; humanity emerging from nature— or perhaps regressing?

It's tiny, about 4 inches high, but it feels quite sturdy. I'm not going to tell Per. I think he'll think it's stupid. I've put it in my pocket. I want to take it home with me after the trip, maybe frame it or mount it at home.

I've just looked up to check on the weather. It's cloudy, but warm, and a little muggy. There's a bird wheeling overhead. It looks like the same bird as the one above us yesterday, but I can't be sure from down here. It's behaving similarly, circling overhead, above the clearing where we are. The sight of the sky above and the little, moving speck makes me feel momentarily dizzy.

"I mark the flowers, ere their prime..."

This is almost funny. I got so sick of Dylan glaring at me disapprovingly when I looked at the map that I gave up and went off without a route. We're at the river now, in the valley. It's about twelve metres wide where we are, and so fast-flowing that it's like being stood next to a motorway. The nearest bridge is on the main E-road, twenty miles southeast, a day's walk there and a day's walk back in the wrong direction.

Dylan is furious, but of course he won't admit that he's angry with me because he has to be so fucking reasonable all the fucking time. He got more and more frustrated as it dawned on him that we'd lost two days walking, until he finally gritted his teeth and said 'I think we should have a break.' So here we are, both sat down on rocks, angrily scribbling in our journals and not talking to each other. I wish someone else were here to see this.

In the valley itself, the ground is boggy and there are pools of green surface water under the knots of undergrowth. It took about four hours to walk five miles to the river, with t-shirts over our mouths, snorting midges out through our noses. They're everywhere; dancing in front of my eyes like a concussion, and making the air in the distance look discoloured. When we were teenagers and we used to camp out by the lake at home, we used to smoke cigarettes and try and ward the midges away with the smoke. I can't remember if it ever worked, although I can remember discovering that you can still inhale smoke even with a t-shirt pulled up over your mouth.

The undergrowth is thick enough to fight back against us as we try and shoulder through. Everything is over-grown, wet, hot and over-fertile in the stinking air. The tip of some sort of flower brushed past me and left sticky pollen on my shoulder, and it made me shudder like some great big glistening phallus had just touched me. Ah, the great outdoors.

I don't even know why we've stopped. We're going to have to wade across the river. Both of us know it. In a minute one of us will have to say it.

I'm thinking about Yngve, of course. That's why I'm feeling so bitter.

I remember Yngve once cut his wrist so deeply that he passed out from blood loss. I remember all of us lying to the hospital staff, and now I wonder what would have happened if we'd told them the truth.

I remember Yngve was sacked from his Saturday job because he told a female customer that he would go and masturbate in the stock cupboard after he had finished serving her. The woman told his manager and he was dismissed on the spot. After the woman left Yngve followed her home and pissed through her letterbox and tried to start a fire but it kept going out. I was so ashamed that I wanted to beat him in front of the woman just so she knew that I hadn't brought him up like this. Except, of course, we did bring him up. The police phoned me to bring him home and I had to stop myself from lying about him and saying I didn't know him. It was completely unprovoked. She had just walked into a shop, and because of the way she looked he had followed her home.

I remember Yngve getting beaten up at school by a group of boys, so badly that both his arms were broken and his lung collapsed. We thought he was going to die.

Yngve left us a list of instructions along with that delusional note, but most of what he wanted couldn't be done. We buried him in a non-denominational memorial ground because we didn't think he'd want a church funeral and, as far as I know, there are no burial grounds anywhere for racist, heavy metal fans. He probably would have wanted a fucking longship, or something. I sat in my living room with Greta, and the celebrant sat opposite us, and I gave her Yngve's list and watched her chewing her lip as her little boat began to sink. The she said:

"Mr Åadland, I know this is incredibly difficult for you,

but I don't think we can have the... the flag that Yngve wanted. I'm sorry. I've never had to refuse anyone's requests before..."

"Can you suggest to me any other organizations that would be prepared to comply with my son's last wishes?" I said, defiantly, because Yngve's note was right there in his own handwriting, and because I didn't know what else to do. I hated the celebrant.

"Umm..." she actually considered my question for a moment before realizing exactly what it was that I was asking. Then her face-hardened and she said, "No, Mr Åadland. I don't think there is anywhere, and if there were then I wouldn't know about it. Perhaps the best thing for your family to do, if this is how you want to remember your son, is to hold the funeral with us and then hold a private wake at your own home, with his own choice of decorations there..." And then I began to laugh, at the idea of the secret Nazi-themed wake, all of us goose-stepping around in SS costumes like that British Prince, Yngve's Swastika flag draped over the coffin and the luger, or the copy of *Mein Kampf*, or whatever the fuck else Yngve had stashed away in his locked bedroom, like something out of an eighties sitcom.

"Is there a particular piece of music that... that Yngve would have liked to have played?"

"Yes. It says right there."

"Oh. *Chainsaw...*"

"Gutsfuck. It's called Chainsaw Gutsfuck."

Greta got up, weeping, and said "For fuck's sake, Per " as she slammed the door.

I remember Chainsaw Gutsfuck buzzing out of the speakers under the stacks of flowers in the non-denominational chapel. It sounded like road traffic, and I turned around and found that nearly all the mourners had got up and left the funeral. There was no-one Yngve's own age at the funeral to have shared his last joke with. I remember thinking how much Yngve must have hated us.

Dylan is staring into the distance, but at least he's not trying to talk about the view or Vikings or something. I'm actually glad his mood has soured a notch. I don't want to talk about fucking trees. Occasionally he pulls that little bundle of twigs out of his pocket and looks it over, and then squirrels it away again when he notices me looking. It looks like a little wooden doll. The way the wires cut into the soft wood and leave behind red rust looks unnervingly like something that's been tied up and bleeding. I wish he'd throw it away.

...that such a sable track

Lay along the grasses green...

Dylan's Journal:10/05/2011, Evening, the second peak

We reached the second peak today. Per has barely said a word to me all day. I really feel like he should have apologized for making that mistake with the map earlier. It would have cost us the whole holiday if we had had to turn back. I'll try and talk to him about it. I know he's had a terrible time recently with Yngve, but he needs to realize that this attitude he has got into recently isn't going to help him to move on, especially not if it ends with him pushing away his friends like this. It's not his fault. He must be in a very selfish place at the moment.

The walk today was more of a chore than anything else. We hit some sort of marshland in the valley, which I don't think either of us was expecting. The trees thinned out a little, but what seemed like mossy ground was actually waterlogged and slippery underfoot. The midges were so thick that I didn't want to breathe.

I am dehydrated, despite all the damp. My eyelids feel heavy, as if I was drunk. We stink, which I suppose is not surprising, but for some reason it's really annoying me. It's like there's this stench following us around, and every time we stop I begin to smell it again and have to keep moving. It's making me really irritable. After wading across the river my clothes were heavy with the water and began to rub away at my waist and knees and where my rucksack straps cross my chest. I had a look under my t-shirt just now and my skin is red and beginning to blister in places. I'll feel a lot more positive when we manage to reach our base camp and relax a bit

But the peak... my first view of the fjord took my breath away. At the very sight of it, the temperature seemed to drop noticeably just from the sheer volume of cold water sucking the heat out of the air. The sides of the cliffs and the slope in front of us are bare of trees, black rock, jagged where they look as though they've been gouged. After the thick forest, seeing the empty water is like coming through the front door after a long commute. It's cold and refreshing, like turning over the pillow in the night.

The water is the sky, blank and unreadable, and the rock is jagged, and huge, the way a parent looks to a tiny child

But I'm so tired. I look back at the forest, and ahead, north, at the next mountain, and I can't help feeling like we've come too far. We're stranded. My legs ache. I can't imagine the effort it will take us to walk all the way back. I feel like I could just lie down here forever.

I'm still thinking about my little stick sculpture. I was thinking about putting it in the garden when I got home, sticking it into the lawn or maybe building some sort of little plinth to put it on under one of the trees. It seems more appropriate somehow, rather than bringing it into the house and domesticating it. The best thing to do would be to bury it, under the lawn. I know that might seem a little bit eccentric, but it just feels so perfect. I feel a certain sort of empathy with whoever made it. Burying it in the ground feels like the ultimate sort of *return to nature*—I know it's just empty symbolism, but then symbolic is what the object is. I took it out of my pocket just now and held it upside down and it looked like a little model of a tree. Planting it would be like allowing it to grow. It would feel wrong, unappreciative, not to do the right thing.

...and the flowers he had tied

As I mark'd, not always died

Sooner than their mates, and yet...

I saw Yngve, up at the peak. Dylan turned to look at me, but didn't say anything, and just for a moment Yngve was stood behind him, leaning over his shoulder, his white-blonde hair in his eyes, smirking at me. I feel sick.

* * *

...their fall was fuller of regret

Dylan has gone.

I'm sat under

~~I don't~~

I don't understand what has happened.

I'm writing this in my journal and then reading it back to myself. I'm waiting for it to fall into place, and then, *click*, I'll get it.

~~I'm sat down trying to~~

~~I need to~~

I'm sat down on the shore of the fjord and I have to write this before I forget it. People will ask me what happened and I need to know.

Dylan is ~~gone d~~
I didn't see him surface from the

I know that what happened ~~can't~~
Just write the words.
Dylan is dead.

Dylan has disappeared. I'm calmer now. I don't think he is dead, really. Realistically. I'm going to write this before I forget to see if I can figure it out, and to keep myself calm. Then I'm going to call mountain rescue.

This is what I saw. We came down the second peak, towards the fjord, and the temperature dropped so severely that I could see my breath in the air. The southern slope we had hiked up had been wooded, but for some reason the northern slope was completely bare. It was silent, too, in the valley. I hadn't realized how noisy the forests had been, with the rasping and buzzing of insects and shudder of moving undergrowth and screams of crows, until we reached the peak and began to climb down. It was so quiet that when rocks tumbled down the mountainside in front of us we could hear them crack apart, and echo from one cliff face to the next.

Like I said, there were no trees on that slope. The rock and soil are so loose it's like walking on ash. Below us, as we slid down, the water seemed impossibly deep even at the shore. The shoreline itself is pitted with wide, flat stones that the water, deep water, runs between like veins of fat in meat, slate grey against black rock. From above, this almost looks like a honeycomb pattern, although less regular. Then the rocks grow less and less frequent, out into the open water. At the edge of the fjord were a small jetty and a few little wooden rowing boats, stretching out into the sea.

The water was painfully cold, not like a southern spring at all but like Tromsø in winter. In the valley, we could no longer see the sun.

Dylan rowed us out into the water. I don't know why, but we argued, and somewhere out on the boat, he said something to me about how I had failed Yngve as a parent. I thought we had reached the far edge of the water, we had been rowing for hours, but when I looked around we were in the very centre of the fjord, between the two shores, over the open water itself. When I didn't respond to Dylan, I didn't know what to say, he began to shake me by my shoulders and scream. I remember trying not to look at him, looking past him, and suddenly I saw that the great, jagged rocks of the cliffs were so distant that I could scarcely make them out from the clouds. Dylan's screams echoed around the silent water, the return echo coming terribly slowly, as if it knew I was waiting for it, from a distance far, far larger than the fjord had looked from the land.

I fell and cracked my ribs on the edge of the boat. My face hung a few feet from the water. I looked down.

The water was a void, like space, bigger than planets. The dark sea seemed to me, in that moment, to be horrifically clear. My stomach lurched, as if I could see down hundreds of metres, miles even, as if I was being suspended over some chasm and I was about to fall. My head span, and I was sick into the water. Then Dylan grabbed the back of my jacket and hauled me back into the boat.

I saw something drifting away on the water. It was Dylan's wooden doll that had been hidden under our tent. It must have slid out of his pocket into the fjord, and it was moving away from the boat, drifting, a little faster than wood should drift on water without waves. On that huge fjord, it looked tiny, insignificant, like something dead.

Dylan cried out when he saw it. He took off his jacket and backpack. I grabbed his waist but he fought me off. He shouted out again, furiously, at me, as if it was my fault, and said something like "I have to bury him." Then he threw himself into the water.

I saw the soles of his feet turned up towards me, kicking limply and pushing him deeper down, under the water, further and further until he had become part of the murk beneath the still surface.

I feel calmer for writing that. Dylan may have swum to shore somewhere. I know I am scared and it's hard to think clearly in situations like this. I am assuming the worst here by jumping to the conclusion that he must have drowned. He might have swum back to the far shore. After all, there's no way I would have seen him if he had. He could have washed up anywhere.

I'm sat on the shore, on the pebbles, on the roots of a tree. I can't tell if I am looking up at the sky or back down into the still sea.

BEN STALLWOOD

It seem'd so hard, and dismal thing

Death, to mark them in the Spring

Greta,

Once again, I'm sorry to have had to send these entries to you. I hope that you feel that it was right for me to have done so, and not that I have meddled unnecessarily and reopened old wounds that you had hoped were healed.

I'm deeply sorry for the loss of your son. As I understand it, Per is now 'lost' to you in a sense as well. I feel Dylan's disappearance every day. I contacted the Norwegian police who had been working on his case, and they said they had already interviewed Per extensively and seen these entries already. I've been looking at maps, and think I might have found the Fjord that Per says Dylan disappeared in, but there is nothing else I can do.

I don't understand why he did what he did. What happened has left me with so many questions to which there are no answers that I find it hard now to trust in anything that I thought I understood.

I've actually wanted to write to you for some time, now. I don't know why, but I feel like the two of us are somehow connected by what happened. I don't know anyone else who could possibly understand what my family has been through, except for you. Please, if only out of pity, will you reply to this letter?

I don't mind what you write. I just want to have a sense of who you are. What did you do before opening this letter? What do you do for a living? What do you look like?

I feel like knowing you will somehow bring me closer to Dylan, to what happened on the fjord that day. Perhaps I can help lift some of the burden of your loss, too.

There is nothing I wouldn't give, just to understand why Dylan did what he did.

Yours,

Emily Pilditch

ABOUT THE AUTHORS

KAREN BOVENMYER

Karen Bovenmyer earned an MFA in Creative Writing: Popular Fiction from the University of Southern Maine. She teaches and mentors students at Iowa State University and serves as the Nonfiction Assistant Editor of Escape Artists' *Mothership Zeta Magazine*. She is the 2016 recipient of the Horror Writer's Association Mary Wollstonecraft Shelley Scholarship. Her short stories and poems appear in more than 20 publications and her first novel will be available Spring 2017.

http://karenbovenmyer.com/

S. L. EDWARDS

S. L. Edwards is a Texan-turned-Californian. He enjoys dark fiction, dark poetry and darker beer. He works on bringing the encroaching horrors of the real world into contact with those of the written word. His fiction has appeared in *Ravenwood Quarterly*, *Turn to Ash*, *Weirdbook*, and *New Zenith Magazine*.

BRIT JONES

After nearly thirty years spent as a working musician, the depredations of effort and time took their toll on Brit Jones, so he returned to his first love: writing short fiction, particularly in the supernatural horror genre. He has been published in the *Onyx Neon Shorts Horror Collection 2015* anthology and *The Helix Literary Journal*. Brit lives in Austin, TX with his wife, two children and three dogs.

JEREMY HEPLER

Native to the Texas Panhandle, I'm a stay-at-home dad and a member of the HWA. In the past six years, I've had twenty-three short stories published in periodicals, anthologies, and online. Most recently, I placed second in the Texas Panhandle Professional Writer's Short Story Competition. My debut novel, *The Boulevard Monster*, will be published by Bloodshot Books in the spring of 2017.

Find me on https://www.facebook.com/jeremy.hepler.5 or https://twitter.com/JeremyHepler to learn more.

MICHELLE ANN KING

Michelle Ann King was born in East London and now lives in Essex. Her stories have appeared in over seventy different venues, including *Interzone*, *Strange Horizons*, and *Black Static*. Her first collection, *Transient Tales*, is available in ebook and paperback now. See www.transientcactus.co.uk for details.

JOSEPH RUBAS

Joseph Rubas is the author of over 200 short stories and several novels. His work has appeared in *The Horror Zine*, *All Due Respect*, *Thuglit*, and others. He is the editor of *The Third Spectral Book of Horror Stories;* additional volumes are forthcoming.

BEN STALLWOOD

Ben Stallwood writes literary and genre fiction, and has been published in markets as diverse as Corvus Review and Dark Chapter Press. He also edits *Empty Oaks*; an up-and-coming spec fic zine. In the real world, Ro lives in Bristol, UK, and works in adult care.

OTHER BOOKS BY ONYX NEON PRESS

Cifiscape Volume I: The Twin Cities by various

Cifiscape Volume II: The Twin Cities by various

Liftoff: Launching Agile Teams & Projects
by Diana Larsen and Ainsley Nies

Onyx Neon Shorts: Horror Collection - 2015

Onyx Neon Shorts: End of The Year Collection - 2014

Dream Walker by Kevin Horwitz

OTHER SHORTS BY ONYX NEON PRESS

2014

2015

For more info on Onyx Neon Shorts, the work we do, or a list of our shorts please visit us online at
http://shorts.onyxneon.com